The Chronicles of Avantia

With special thanks to Cherith Baldry

To JJ, a big fan

www.chroniclesofavantia.com

ORCHARD BOOKS
338 Euston Road, London NW1 3BH
Orchard Books Australia
Level 17/207 Kent St, Sydney, NSW 2000

A Paperback Original
First published in Great Britain in 2010

Chronicles of Avantia is a registered trademark of Beast Quest Limited
Series created by Working Partners Limited, London

Text © Beast Quest Limited 2010
Cover and inside illustrations by Artful Doodlers, with special thanks
to Bob and Keiron. © Orchard Books 2010

A CIP catalogue record for this book is available from
the British Library.

ISBN 978 1 40830 747 2

9 10 8

Printed in Great Britain By CPI Bookmarque, Croydon

The paper and board used in this paperback are natural recyclable
products made from wood grown in sustainable forests.
The manufacturing processes conform to the environmental
regulations of the country of origin.

Orchard Books is a division of Hachette Children's Books,
an Hachette UK company.

www.hachette.co.uk

First Hero

By Adam Blade

ORCHARD BOOKS

www.chroniclesofavantia.com

The gathering of the Beasts

Prologue

Deep in the belly of the volcano, my talons grip the baking rock. I sense liquid fire bubbling, heat rising: this is my birthplace.

Dawn is near. An event long awaited is about to begin. I must act; I feel it from my talons to the tips of my shimmering wings.

I take to the air. My powerful wings lift me into the swirling hot currents and I rise out of the crater in a burst of flame. I hover in the cool night air, letting the breeze ruffle my feathers. I look out over my homeland: Avantia.

Out there is my destiny. My Chosen Rider. At last it is time to find him.

I open my beak and let out a cry that echoes between valleys and trees; my signal, sent out to trusted friends. It is many moons since we last met. I settle onto the volcano's crater to wait.

I spot a tiny shape in the distance, far above me, moving swiftly against the lightening sky. Excitement races through me. The shape grows larger, until it takes the form of...a grey wolf. He dives towards me. At the last moment he opens his leathery wings and lands gently on four strong legs. He paces around the edge of the crater. I nod my head in recognition. Gulkien has come.

An eerie yowl cleaves the air. From the shadows pooled at the volcano's foot appears a huge, puma-like cat, lithe and agile, bounding over boulders towards the summit. Sparks fly as her claws rake the rocks. Her fur is golden and her amber eyes flash in the volcano's fires. Here is Nera. I know her of old – her fierce courage will be needed in the testing times ahead. It fills me with pleasure to see my friend return.

From the other side of the crater comes a slithering sound. I turn to see the great serpent, Falkor, emerge from a vast fissure in the rock, his forked tongue flicking the air, tasting it. The flames from the lava-filled crater reflect on his scaly form as he winds his way towards us, his body pulsing with muscular energy. Colours swirl on his flanks, like spilt oil in water. His wide head, bristling with spines, bows in greeting. Nothing – neither stars nor fire – reflects in his black eyes. Falkor folds his shining coils around a boulder, alert and waiting.

My feathers blaze more brightly. This is a momentous day: we have come together again. I open my wings to their widest extent. The Beasts come closer, bowing their heads to listen. The air crackles with energy, as if a storm is about to break.

It is time, I tell them. *Our enemy of old, Derthsin, brings danger to the kingdom. War is brewing. We must each find our Chosen Rider.*

Gulkien throws back his head and unleashes a howl that reverberates around the volcano's slopes. Nera joins in with a thunderous growl – I feel the rocks beneath us creak and shift. Falkor hisses and tightens his coils around the boulder, causing a crack to spread. My own exultant cry erupts from deep within my throat.

Gulkien leaps into the air, beating his wings savagely. I watch him speed away. Nera bounds down the rocky slopes to disappear into the shadows. Falkor stretches his body out to its full glittering length, bows his head to me in farewell, and slithers into a fissure.

Good luck, my friends. My thoughts are with you.

Last of all, I spread out my wings, feeling their power, and take to the air.

I am Firepos, and my Chosen Rider is waiting...

I fly, watching the land as it speeds beneath me in a blurred patchwork of crop fields and dark woodlands.

Rolling hills stretch far ahead – hulking shadows beneath the pre-dawn sky. At their feet, undulating in the breeze like a black sea, is a vast pine forest. Beyond the trees lurk bleak, fog-shrouded moors, and then a wide grassy plain. Smoke curls up from the villages that are scattered over the land like seeds. The ocean is like a silver thread to the west.

All seems quiet in the world...

I smell smoke. Smoke, and something else... My feathers glow in anguish: it is the odour of charred flesh. Human flesh. Ahead I spy a flickering orange glow.

Fire.

I swoop down, gliding over the dense forest. My talons brush the leaves of the tallest trees. I see cornfields bathed in an angry wash of flame, and thatched huts billowing smoke. The village of Forton is under attack!

Screams rend the air over the inferno's roar. Invaders in battle-scarred armour storm the streets, scattering villagers before them. Spear tips and swords glint, many dripping with blood. I see a few villagers turn to fight, but they are cut down without mercy. The streets are littered with bodies.

Deep in my core, my senses stir. He is here somewhere: my Chosen Rider.

I should have come sooner. What if I am too late?

I hover over the woods near the edge of the village, bristling with anxiety. All I can do is wait, and watch...

A sweat-streaked warhorse canters down the track from the village. On its back rides a giant of a warrior. His body is encased in close-fitting black armour, adorned with spikes. A cloak the colour of dried blood hangs over his broad shoulders and at his hip hangs a bronze-hilted sword. His face is obscured by a leathery mask – misshapen and ugly. My feathers tingle.

That mask. I know it...

Spikes jut from its dangling jowls and its gaping jaws

are lined with pointed teeth. Two horns curl up from its
temples, ending in wicked barbs like fish hooks. It is the
face of a Dark Beast, a near-mythical creature called
Anoret, which stalked the land many years ago. The mask
is an artefact of great power.

The Face of Anoret, also known to the people of Avantia
as the Mask of Death.

And the rider – it is Derthsin!

I tip my wings and swoop down with a cry of fury.

Derthsin twists around in his saddle to face me. I
channel flames towards my talons – a fireball gathers in
strength and intensity. Soon this enemy will be a heap of
smouldering ashes…

I see his eyes glitter through the holes in his grotesque
mask. With a casual flick, he waves his hand at me.

It feels as though I'm caught in a hurricane. An invisible
force smashes into me and hurls me off my attack course.
The ground rushes up. Too quickly…

With a screech, I crash into a cornfield. The fireball in
my talons bursts around me, scorching the corn and lighting
up the night. My wings buckle, bones at breaking point.

Through the haze of pain, I understand: the myth of the Face of Anoret is true! It bestows power over the Beasts of Avantia to the wearer.

My fear grows – I am unprepared for this fight. I try to move, but I cannot: Derthsin still holds me in his thrall.

As I lie helpless and hidden from view, a man runs along the track towards the warrior. Dressed in rough woollen jerkin and leggings, he carries a farmer's thresher: two pieces of wood joined with a chain. Behind the man chases a small boy, his tear-streaked face framed with brown hair.

My senses blaze. It is my Chosen Rider! I struggle to get up, but still I cannot move.

The boy grasps the man's hand and tries to pull him back. His face is stricken with fear. The man shakes him off. 'Go and hide in the woods, son!' He turns towards the warrior, who has dismounted and drawn his long, wicked-looking sword.

With a cry of rage, the man charges at Derthsin, raising his thresher and aiming a clumsy swipe at his head.

Derthsin neatly sidesteps, allowing his attacker to pass

by. A noise like laughter comes from the mask, the sound distorted and ugly. With the speed of a striking snake he closes on the villager and raises his sword to strike...

The man ducks beneath the swinging blade, and as he stands up he swings the thresher — more by luck than judgement — into Derthsin's head. Derthsin bellows in anger as the mask is torn from his face. He falls to his knees and drops his sword. The villager kicks it away.

I feel Derthsin's hold over me fade, but I am still too weak to move.

I can see his dark features: thin, bloodless lips, a heavy brow looming over deep-set black eyes, and a strong nose. A thin trail of blood trickles down his cheek. He stares at the farmer. One more swing of the thresher will kill him.

'Think carefully,' Derthsin says. His voice is soft but commanding. He glances at the boy. 'Do you want your son to see you kill an unarmed man?'

The man turns and shouts back to my Chosen Rider. 'Get away! Hide! Find your mother...'

Derthsin's hand creeps to a sheath on his belt. He draws out a long dagger.

I struggle to get up.

In two long strides Derthsin closes on the man. Moonlight flashes on steel. The man groans as the blade slides between his ribs. The thresher hits the ground.

Someone else approaches, stumbling down the road from Forton. A woman, crying in anguish. She bends over the stricken villager, cradling his head in her arms. A band of jeering soldiers follows in her wake.

'Put her in the cart with the rest,' Derthsin orders. The soldiers drag the screaming woman back to the village.

Derthsin picks up my Chosen Rider by his collar and stares into his eyes. The boy struggles, legs and fists flailing.

'I sense strength in your soul,' Derthsin growls. 'But death is stronger than you.' He raises his knife, pointing it at the boy's heart.

I turn my feathers the colour of coal and silently take to the air. I circle once and swoop at the murderous warrior.

The boy's mouth opens in a silent scream.

I plunge my talons into Derthsin's shoulders and lift him off the ground. He drops the boy and roars as I carry him up into the air. I feel him writhing in my grasp, but I will not let go. Not yet.

Over the forest and plains I fly. Ahead I spy the glow of my volcano. He must know now where I mean to take him, for his roars become screams. Over the crater, the heat blasts us. In the depths, the pool of molten rock bubbles.

'You'll pay for this!' Derthsin roars.

With a victorious screech, I let him go. His hand grips one of my feathers, but I twist, and the feather tears away. It doesn't slow his fall. His body tumbles and spins as he plunges through the air. The lava swallows him, cutting off his screams.

I soar back to Forton, which is still ablaze. The soldiers are scattering, searching for their leader. Dark smoke billows across the road. The boy leans over his father. The smoke sweeps past him, but he doesn't seem to notice. Beside him is the Mask of Death.

I land on the road and gently nuzzle the boy. He throws his arm around my neck and sobs into my warm feathers. He can feel our bond. He is young and fragile and his future is uncertain. Is he strong enough to face it?

I must do all I can to help him. But for now we must heal our wounds.

Stay strong, I will the boy. Your destiny awaits you. From the dark, a hero must rise.

Tanner summons Firepos from the Stonewin volcano

Chapter One

Angry skies and the clash of swords filled Tanner's dreams. A harsh cry sounded out and he felt himself being torn from sleep, rushing up to the surface of consciousness. His eyelashes fluttered open. He realised that the cry that woke him had come from his own lips. Moonlight flooded through the window. He sat up and dragged a weary hand across his eyes. His dream lingered in his thoughts, threatening and deadly.

With a sigh, he threw off his blankets and scrambled out of bed, wincing as his feet touched the cold floor. He pushed his long hair out of his eyes and splashed cold water from a tin basin onto his face. Feeling more awake, he pulled his tunic over his head and tugged on his battered old boots.

He looked out of the window. Light gathered on the horizon, glowing on the rough track that led to Forton. To the north, in the direction of Harron, he saw a faint orange glow. *A bonfire, perhaps?* Tanner wondered. He gazed at his reflection in the dirty windowpane. Long brown hair framed his pale face. Above high cheekbones, his dark eyes betrayed last night's troubled sleep.

I'm late for work, he thought. No time for breakfast. He crept past his grandmother's room and smiled as he heard her soft snores. Quietly opening the front door, he stepped into the cold morning. The air misted as he took a few deep breaths. Tanner smelt mint drifting from the well-tended herb garden. The plants had been crushed by something large, and some of the leaves were charred at the edges. 'That won't make grandmother very happy,' he muttered, smiling. He knew who the culprit was!

His route to the bakery in Forton where he worked led down the path behind a row of thatched cottages, not far from the edge of the woods where his father had been killed and his mother abducted. It was hard to believe that eight years had passed since that terrible day. The memory of it was as raw as ever: the anguish of his dying father's face, his mother's screams as she was dragged away.

Tanner shook his head and ran to the bakery.

*

Heat blasted over Tanner's body as he sucked in the scorching air. Sweat poured off him, even though he was stripped to the waist. Although not yet fully grown, Tanner was lithe, nimble and stronger than he looked.

Using the long-handled paddle, he took the last loaves from the oven and laid them to rest on the cooling racks. He put a couple of loaves under his arm, waved goodbye to the baker – who still had a day of selling bread ahead of him – and stepped into Forton's village square. In the hours since he had started work, it had filled with people. The sun had risen over the rooftops, and shutters were opening to the smell of fresh bread.

Tanner stood for a moment, raising his face to the sun. A washerwoman hurried past with bundles of clean linen under her arms. A fisherman and his son, Ben, balanced a pole strung with trout across their shoulders.

'Stop by our stall later,' Ben called to Tanner. 'I'll have some fried fish for you, in exchange for bread.'

Tanner grinned at Ben and lifted a hand in acknowledgement. After the loss of his parents he had thought there was nothing to live for, but time had gone some way to heal the wound. He had many friends in the village. And his grandmother, although grumpy and short-tempered, looked after him. *Life could be worse*, he always told himself, when he felt sad.

Tanner looked at the stout wooden palisade topped with sharpened stakes, and the shallow dry moat surrounding Forton. Defences had been added when Forton was rebuilt after Derthsin's attack. Despite the protection, fear of violence remained – Avantia was a dangerous place, with no ruler. Warbands roamed the lands, raiding villages, and bandits prowled the quieter stretches of road.

Forton was prepared for invasions. Everyone was expected to know how to fight. Over the years, an uneasy calm had settled over the village – people remembered Derthsin, but his presence had not been felt for years. Everyone assumed he was dead.

Tanner made his way home, striding through the stockade gate, over the moat bridge and onto the track. His day's work was not over; he still had to look after his beloved grandmother.

In the kitchen, Tanner prodded the embers of the fire into life and hung a huge black kettle over it. When the kettle was singing, he made his grandmother's morning herb tea and took it to her with a plate of the fresh bread and some butter.

Grandmother Esme was already sitting up in bed, a multicoloured shawl around her shoulders. She eyed him impatiently as she tied up her unruly grey dreadlocks with a scrap of scarlet linen. Tanner set the tray down on the bed and kissed her on the cheek; her skin felt paper-thin, and the circles under her eyes were darker than ever.

'Bring me my box of oracle bones, boy,' she said.

Tanner groaned. 'Fortune telling again?'

His grandmother's face clouded. 'Change is coming to Avantia. I must read the bones so we can prepare ourselves. Now do as you're told!'

Tanner felt a chill crawl over his skin. As he went to fetch the box, he thought back to his troubled dreams.

Something was brewing. Could Grandmother Esme's pieces of bone spell out the future? Her fortune-telling was renowned in the village, and she made a small living reading people's palms. *There's no denying it*, he thought grimly. *One way or another, they always seem to help her see what's coming.*

As Tanner returned to his grandmother's room and set the box down on the bed, he heard the sound of hooves coming from the north road. Esme looked up with watery eyes.

'Wait here,' said Tanner. He snatched up his sword from the rack at the front door and walked into the road, shielding his eyes from the sun. He saw a cloud of dust coming along the track. A single horseman. Tanner let out the breath he had been holding: it was Drew, a farmer who worked the land further outside the village boundary.

But as the horse drew closer, Tanner's anxiety

returned. Drew wobbled in the saddle, and his head was bowed forward. His horse's flanks were slick with sweat. Twenty paces away, Drew slumped against his horse's mane. Tanner gasped when he saw the black-fletched arrow protruding from his back. The horse came to a halt and Drew slid from the saddle.

Tanner rushed to help him up. He blanched at the sticky red blood staining Drew's tunic, stark against his deathly pale skin. Tanner heaved him up onto his shoulder and dragged him to the cottage.

Esme appeared in the doorway. 'I'll get water,' she said, 'and bandages.' She disappeared back into the gloom of the cottage.

'What happened?' asked Tanner, helping the farmer sit down on the front step and lean his shoulder against the doorframe.

Drew sucked in a shallow breath. 'An army,' he gasped. 'Hundreds of men marching this way.'

'What army?' said Tanner. No armies had marched in Avantia since Derthsin had disappeared. Bandits prowled the land, but not armies.

Drew shook his head. 'I don't know. Not just soldiers. Some sort of creature...' He choked and flecks of blood gathered around his lips. 'They destroyed Harron town last night. They murdered everyone. It was just like the last time...'

Dread ran down Tanner's spine.

'I tried to escape, but one of their scouts shot me... Some brute riding a varkule—' Drew broke off, coughing up more blood.

'Don't speak any more,' Tanner said. 'Try to save your strength.'

Tanner's grandmother hobbled over with a bowl of hot water and clean strips of linen.

'Drew says soldiers are coming,' said Tanner, his voice tight with tension.

His grandmother's glance shifted to the doorway leading back into the house. Tanner swallowed. Surely no one could know what was hidden beneath the floorboards? The fragment of the Mask of Death was their secret.

One piece was buried beneath their home, while the other pieces were scattered across the kingdom. Esme had never told Tanner where they were, or why she hadn't destroyed them. 'It's not for you to know,' she would say, shaking her head. 'Not yet.' After a few years, Tanner had stopped asking about the pieces of the mask. Until today, he'd almost forgotten about them.

'Grandmother,' Tanner said, putting his hand on her arm. 'I have to go and look.'

She turned her shrewd gaze on him and nodded grimly. She pressed a damp cloth against Drew's bloody wound. He gasped with pain. 'Be careful. And remember all you have learnt these past years.'

Tanner rushed round to the back of the cottage, his heart thumping, and scrambled up the small plateau between the trees. He looked east, towards the distant volcano that still spewed lava several times a year.

Cupping his mouth, he called the name of his most trusted friend.

'Firepos!' Tanner's voice echoed up towards the distant peak.

A shape burst from the volcano's glowing mouth, spreading mighty red-brown wings. Tanner's fear receded as the great Beast soared towards him, driving through the Avantian morning with powerful strokes. The Flame Bird was silhouetted against the sun, her sharp beak shining as she sliced through the air. Firepos drew close, thrusting out her talons to land gently in front of him. Gold shimmered among her ruffled feathers, and he felt the heat rising from her flanks.

'Are you ready?' he said.

Firepos replied with a shrill call, and lowered her body. Tanner climbed onto her back and clutched the thick feathers behind her head.

'North!' he shouted.

The Dragon Warrior and his army march on Forton

Chapter Two

Firepos soared over the cottage. The green plains and rocky mountains of Avantia swept into view. It looked peaceful, but so vulnerable. Sleepy villages and open fields were no defence against attacking armies.

Even with these doubts prickling inside him, Tanner felt a thrill of exhilaration as they took to the sky. The first time he and Firepos had flown together had been the day after his father's murder and mother's abduction. He'd been terrified, clinging to her plumage and burying his face in her neck, unable to look down. He couldn't understand why this Beast had chosen him to be her rider.

But as the seasons passed, and then the years, their bond had grown and strengthened like the roots of a tree. After a while, he stopped questioning why. He trusted his Beast above all others, and he knew they were meant to be together. *When the time is right, Firepos will let me know why she chose me.*

Firepos had been a patient trainer. Tanner wasn't sure what he was being trained for, and when he tried to ask, his Beast would close her eyes and wait for the questions to cease. For a long while he hadn't been sure if Firepos understood him, until he realised that she could read his thoughts.

He learnt how to hold on to the Beast's back during her steepest dives, how to live on a mountainside without dying of exposure, and where to hunt in the most barren places. He was no longer the skinny seven-year-old who'd watched his father die. He was stronger now, in body and spirit. Firepos had taught him how to survive.

Now Firepos flew high across a hill, her wings spread wide. Astride her back, Tanner surveyed the expanse of green pasture to the west, and the gleaming waters of the lake to the east, where Ben and his father fished. To the north, over the plains, the peaks were cold blue smears on a hazy horizon. Tanner had flown between those peaks many times, numbed by hail and freezing winds.

The whistle of the wind sang in his ears and his eyes watered, but as they pushed through a low-hanging cloud, tearing through drifting white, he experienced the excitement he always felt when flying on Firepos's back. He sensed the steady beat of Firepos's wings and the strong thump of her heart. She responded to his unspoken commands, cutting through the rough air, buffeted in the wild aerial winds.

The Beast's flight settled and she dropped out of the clouds. The road leading to Forton stretched beneath them, winding its way through the hills. In the distance, Tanner saw a cloud of dust rising from the road. He bade Firepos fly lower as they approached. *We must stay out of sight*, he urged her.

They closed on the dust cloud. What Tanner saw next chilled his blood.

Down the road tramped three columns of soldiers, one behind the other, the disciplined trudge of their march carrying up to him. At the four points of each column, outriders rode on the back of varkules – giant, hyena-like creatures the size of horses, with mottled hides and sharp tusks. Streaks of thick fur lined their spines, ears were pointed and alert, nostrils sniffing the air for prey. One of them cried out, and Tanner shuddered at the faint noise of the animal's howl.

Leading the advance, mounted on a magnificent black stallion, was a tall man dressed in black armour that glinted and flashed. Tanner couldn't see his features. His helmet, shaped like the snout of a dragon, was firmly shut. Everything about the Dragon Warrior was dark; he seemed to suck the light from around him. A cold sensation trickled through Tanner's chest. There was something dreadful in the purpose of the men's march.

'Lower, Firepos,' Tanner murmured.

They made a pass over the army. 'There must be three hundred at least,' he said. He saw that the soldiers wore full leather body armour. The leading elements carried spears, and swords hung at their sides. Behind them came men with long-handled battle-axes resting on their shoulders, and bringing up the rear marched a contingent of crossbowmen. Their helmets hid most of their faces, but their mouths were cruel and hard.

Tanner flew overhead, casting a dark shadow over the army. The Dragon Warrior reined in his stallion and shouted a command. The rest of the soldiers stopped dead as the crossbowmen rushed out of the column, rapidly forming a line, two-men deep. The front rank went down on their knees, aiming their weapons at Firepos.

Fear choked Tanner's throat.

I have to warn everyone! Firepos tipped back her head and soared higher.

'Loose!' bellowed the Dragon Warrior. There was a clatter as the crossbowmen shot their bolts. Missiles whistled past Firepos, several passing through the feathers in her tail. She beat her wings harder and flew out of range.

Tanner twisted round, gazing down towards his village. The palisade would be no defence against these men, with their varkules and iron discipline. Firepos let out a cry as they darted between the clouds and Tanner brought his chest close to her body. *Quick, Firepos!* Reassurance radiated up to him from her warm feathers.

After so many years our time has come. All the lessons I have taught Tanner will be put to the test. I have done everything I can to prepare him. But I sense his fear. I only hope he has the strength to survive. If he fails, I will have sent him to his death.

Firepos swooped down into Forton's central square, drawing gasps from the villagers trading at the stalls as her talons skittered onto the cobbles. It was market day, so nearly all of Forton was there.

It was the first time for many years that Firepos had shown herself to anyone other than Tanner and Esme. Tanner could feel her trepidation at doing so – she had kept herself a secret for a long time. How would the villagers react to seeing young

Tanner, the baker's apprentice, riding a Beast only mentioned in the old legends of history books?

For a few seconds people stared, opened mouthed, unwilling to believe their eyes. A scream rent the air. Some people scrambled to get away, knocking over piles of fruit and bundles of wool from the stalls, and disappearing down alleys. Parents grabbed their children and hugged them to their chests. Other braver souls simply stared in wonder.

At least not everyone is running away, Tanner thought. *It's probably because they know me. I have to try to explain what is going on.*

Tanner leapt off Firepos's back and ran to the bell in the centre of the square. He seized the rope and yanked on it with all his strength, sending loud peals out over the village. The bell was only to be used as a warning of grave danger. People emerged from their houses, slowly, torn between their curiosity and fear of the Beast. All gazed up at Firepos with wide eyes.

'Do not fear Firepos,' Tanner called. 'She is a

Beast of Legend, and I am her Chosen Rider.'

Murmurs echoed around the square. A few people approached Firepos. She eyed them beadily, unsure of how they would act.

Simon, the village leader – a sensible man who had helped Tanner bury his father – stepped forward from the crowd. 'Hush, everyone,' he said. 'Tanner, what in Avantia is going on?'

Tanner climbed onto Firepos's back and stood up so everyone could hear him. 'Soldiers are coming! Hundreds of them. Break out the weapons. Man the walls!'

'Bandits?' Simon said. 'They wouldn't attack our town. It's too well protected.'

'These are not common bandits, Simon. Our walls will be useless in the face of these men. They have varkules. These men are...' He didn't know how to say it. He looked into his friend's face. 'They'll kill us all. They've already razed Harron to the ground. They nearly killed Drew.'

A murmur of fresh panic rippled through the

villagers. Simon's face darkened. 'All those in the militia, to the armoury. Anyone who can hold a weapon, get ready to fight,' he shouted, looking around. 'Everyone else, into the cellars.' He turned back to Tanner. 'Can you and your Beast help us?'

Tanner's heart pounded as he watched the villagers hurry to the armoury. They emerged with grim faces, carrying crossbows, swords, clubs and axes.

The sound of a war horn blasted from outside the village. Fear closed over Tanner like a black cloud. He felt cold. His hands were wet with sweat.

'Will you help us?' Simon insisted.

'I'll hold them off as long as I can,' Tanner said, swallowing his fear. 'Organise a defence with the time I buy you.'

Simon nodded and ran off, barking orders.

'Go, Firepos,' Tanner cried. 'Head for the fields.'

As the Beast soared away from the village, Tanner's heart thumped even harder. The cruel worm of doubt returned and his stomach tightened. He'd promised to hold off the army, but he'd seen the varkules, the weapons, the deadly intent in every stride the soldiers took towards Forton. He looked down at his thin tunic. One slash of a blade and his heart could be torn from his chest.

But he had a Beast, and they did not! That was something, at least.

'It's our time, Firepos,' he told her. 'Time to defend our home.' He could hear his own voice trembling. He'd seen death before, smelt its scent – death had taken Tanner's father. Now it had returned.

Even with Firepos's training, would Tanner be able to cheat death a second time?

The Beasts begin their battle

Chapter Three

I can feel Tanner's determination fighting with his fear. He steers me in a wide path, behind a copse of trees, and only a wing's length over the ground. I understand: he means to attack the raiders from behind, before they have a chance to muster their defences.

We swoop over a low rise, and there they are. The marching columns with their backs to us. My feathers are alive with flame.

Tanner clung to Firepos as she let out a furious shriek and dived at one of the army's varkule outriders. Tanner drew his sword. At the last second, sensing danger, the varkule's head snapped round.

Tanner leant out from Firepos as far as he dared and, as he passed by, slashed his sword across the rider's chest. The enemy fell with a scream, rolling and tumbling in the dirt.

Adrenalin rushed through Tanner's veins, and he had no time to dwell on what he had just done.

The rear elements of the army broke ranks with anxious shouts. Tanner let out a yell of triumph as Firepos seized up two crossbowmen in her talons. He heard their cries as she dropped them into the midst of the leading column of spearmen. Men sprawled on the ground, limbs snapping like twigs. The Dragon Warrior wheeled around on his stallion. 'Hold firm!' he bellowed.

Many sprinted into the trees on either side of the road. Others crouched and lifted their crossbows, firing wildly at Firepos. A company of spearmen grouped together and pointed their weapons aloft so Firepos couldn't get close.

The varkules reared, but their riders brought them under control. Tanner looped away, readying himself for another pass. He could hear the crackle of flames as his Beast gathered a fireball in her talons. That would soon put them to flight.

As he steered Firepos to face the enemy again, he saw the Dragon Warrior dismount and lay a hand on his stallion's mane. He seemed to whisper something quietly in its ear.

'What's he doing?' Tanner muttered.

The stallion shook its mane as if shaking off a swarm of angry wasps. It lifted its head and snorted. The sound carried all the way to Tanner. It reared up on its hind legs, but instead of falling back to the ground, the creature stayed perfectly balanced. His forelegs started to expand and lengthen. Tanner felt his mouth turn dry. This was no ordinary horse.

The hind legs thickened, growing as wide as tree stumps beneath the horse's massive body. The rear hooves swelled and hardened into bronze, and the front hooves twisted into claws. *Weapons*, Tanner thought. *He's growing weapons!* Lips folded back and shrank. Eyes, alight with intelligence, shifted in its head so that the horse's face looked grotesquely human. The creature's chest heaved and Tanner saw that his glossy coat now stretched across a body more like a man's. Muscles flexed as it raised a hooked claw into the air, slicing.

'It's a Beast!' Tanner shouted over the wind.

*

The fire in my heart flickers as I see him. It is true, then: Varlot exists. In all my days, I've never seen him. They say that Varlot kills without conscience, that he cares nothing for the world around him – that he even refuses a Chosen Rider. So what is he doing with the Dragon Warrior? We have a new enemy, Tanner and I.

Firepos shivered, sending Tanner a message. A name seeped into his consciousness: *Varlot. So that was the name of the Beast.*

The stallion's glossy coat hardened into scales – a cracked layer of bronze covering its entire body. The enemy soldiers gathered in their ranks behind the towering horse-Beast.

Firepos sent another message. *Don't be afraid.*

'I'm not. I can do this,' Tanner muttered, hoping he sounded braver than he felt, and knowing there was no way to fool Firepos. *If I behave like a brave warrior, perhaps I'll become one,* he thought to himself.

There was no time left for thinking. The Flame Bird screeched, blasting a fireball that streaked through the sky like a comet.

Varlot arched back its arms, exposing its chest, threw back its head and roared. The fireball smashed into its armour in an explosion of fire and brimstone. When the smoke cleared, the Beast was still standing, its armour untarnished. It swiped a claw in Tanner's direction, sending out a bellow of defiance.

A spear flashed up from below. Tanner yanked Firepos's feathers, and she darted sideways. The weapon sailed past, but another caught her wing and sent her spinning. Firepos screeched. Tanner gritted his teeth and hung on as the world blurred. When the Beast righted herself, he saw more spearmen taking aim.

'That was too close!' he called to Firepos, pulling her out of range.

Below, the soldiers were regrouping. The Dragon Warrior was directing them down the main road to the village, led by two varkule outriders and Varlot. The Dragon Warrior watched, and then headed off with a few soldiers along the track that led to Tanner's grandmother's cottage. Why was the Dragon Warrior splitting up his forces?

Tanner didn't know whether to follow the main attack, or defend his grandmother. Did he care more for the hundreds of villagers, or the only family he had left? He sensed the Flame Beast waiting for him to make his decision. He glanced after the soldiers, then back towards the Dragon Warrior. Every second he hesitated, danger was edging closer to innocent lives.

Take me down, he urged Firepos, directing his Beast towards the heart of the village. Even as they moved through the air, Tanner still didn't know if he'd made the right decision.

His loyal Beast dipped her beak and dived, shooting fireballs into the path of the marching army. They smashed onto the ground, throwing up clods of earth and billowing smoke. Soldiers screamed, engulfed in flames, rolling on the ground to extinguish them.

I am a killer, Tanner thought with horror. *A few days ago I was just a baker's apprentice. Now I have blood on my hands.*

Pushing this feeling aside, Tanner steered Firepos through the rising black columns and watched the army scatter in disarray. Then he bore down on the enemy Beast. When they were fifty paces away, flying low above the ground, Tanner swung his leg over Firepos's back in a move they'd practised a thousand times before. He jumped, hit the ground and rolled to a halt.

As he leapt up, he saw Firepos descend onto Varlot, raking at his armour, piercing it with her sharp talons. The Beast flailed, but Firepos bravely clung on.

Varlot's eyes glitter with hunger for my blood, but he shall face a fight like no other. He swipes his claws at me, just missing my beak.

Enough! I dart around his body, arching my wings to catch the slightest eddy of air that lifts me above his head, just out of reach. Varlot's mind is closed to me; I cannot read his thoughts. Whoever tamed him has given him the ability to close his mind to other Beasts.

The sun momentarily blinds Varlot and I take my chance, darting in with my beak to slice at his eyes. Varlot cries out, his chest heaving, and he staggers. My enemy falls to the ground. He hasn't the heart to face Firepos the Flame Bird!

Firepos hovered above Varlot. The Dragon Warrior's Beast reared up onto his hind legs and drew his head back, his chest widening as he roared with fury. Claws swiped out at Firepos, but she ducked and swerved in the air, her feathered coat shimmering. The army was marching towards the village, brandishing their glinting weapons.

'Firepos!' Tanner shouted. 'Go to the village. Protect them!'

The Flame Bird screeched and banked away,

flying towards Forton. She clutched a fireball in her talons, ready to attack.

Tanner sprinted down the track towards his grandmother's cottage. He had to get there before the soldiers. He took a shortcut between the trees, leaping over fallen logs and hidden ditches. *Why had the Dragon Warrior come this way? And what would he do when he found grandmother?* Branches and leaves lashed his face as he charged between the trees.

A scream cut through the air and Tanner's heart skipped a beat.

Esme faces the Dragon Warrior

Chapter Four

As Tanner raced towards the cottage, he spotted his grandmother. She stood in the doorway, gripping the axe he used for chopping wood. At her feet a soldier was curled up in the dirt, clutching a hand to his neck. Blood poured out between his fingers as he gazed up at Esme, horrified.

A snarling varkule loomed over her, its rider keeping a firm grip on the reins. The hair along the animal's spine stood erect and his ears were flattened back against his huge head as he snapped his jaws at Esme. Tanner saw her lip curl with disgust at the smell. Beside the animal stood the Dragon Warrior, flanked by three more enemy soldiers, all armed with curved blades.

'Give in, you old witch,' one of them taunted.

She glanced down at the bleeding man who was crawling away from her. 'Give in?' she said incredulously. 'Come here and say that! I'll split your skull open, too.'

The soldier lunged at her angrily.

'Leave her alone!' shouted Tanner, drawing his sword. He ran to his grandmother's side, leaping over the injured soldier who tried to grab his ankles.

'Ah, more peasants to sport with,' smirked the varkule rider.

Esme glared at him. 'Tanner, get behind me,' she snapped, raising her axe.

Rage boiled inside Tanner, and he stepped forwards, slashing at the varkule's chest. The animal reared up and threw off its rider, who cried out as he fell to the ground. Leaping to his feet, the soldier pointed his spear at Tanner.

But the soldier didn't have time to attack — the bleeding varkule lunged, ferocious jaws tearing at Tanner's tunic. Tanner darted to the right, avoiding a second fierce snap of those deadly teeth. The varkule's fur bristled with hostility. Its rider called out an order and the varkule hesitated, spit dripping over Tanner. The animal backed away, licking his gums. Tanner could feel his hands trembling as he held his sword out before him.

The soldier held his cloak against his mount's wound. 'You'll pay for this, boy!'

'Enough!' said a gravelly voice. The Dragon Warrior approached. Tanner saw swirling grooves cut into the surface of the warrior's armour, lined with gold. His face was still covered by the heavy dragon-helmet, but now Tanner could see bright eyes staring through the visor.

The Dragon Warrior drew a deep breath into his nostrils, the distorted sound snorting through the visor. 'She's hiding something. The Mask of Death is close. I can smell it.' He took off his helmet and looked at Tanner's grandmother, who still stood in the doorway with the axe. He took off his helmet. His voice softened. 'Come out, old woman. I want to talk to you.' Esme took a step forwards.

With lightning speed, the Dragon Warrior grabbed her axe in one hand and her throat in the other, pulling her face close to his. 'You know where it is,' he said. 'I see it in your eyes.'

Esme's eyes blazed defiantly as the soldiers surrounded her. 'Your breath is worse than the varkule's,' she said.

'Tell us,' said the Dragon Warrior. 'Or die.'

'She doesn't know where—' Tanner began.

'I'll never tell you,' Esme spat.

The soldiers reach the village. The gate proves no obstacle to the charging varkules. The soldiers run down the roads and alleys to the centre. The defenders of Forton, under the command of Simon, are assembled in the square. Carts have been overturned and they stand behind them, archers and crossbowmen with their weapons levelled, spears and swords gripped.

A volley of arrows cuts down the first enemy wave, but other soldiers storm the square, jumping over their fallen comrades and clambering over the barricades with bloodthirsty cries. Brutal hand-to-hand combat begins, and the villagers fall back under the disciplined fury of the raiders. I cannot use my fireballs – innocent people will be hurt. I swoop down, grasp a soldier in my talons and fling him into his comrades.

More villagers run out of doorways, striking with whatever weapons they can find. A boy shoots his hunting bow, the arrow bursting through an enemy's thigh. As blood pours down the soldier's leg he slashes out angrily with his sword. The cobbles are already slick with blood.

The ground seems to shake and everyone looks up. Varlot strides into the square, and the timber walls of the buildings shudder. The villagers are shocked and afraid. I screech, trying to tell them to run away. They can't face a creature of this size. But Simon waves his arm to keep them in line.

'As I thought,' said the Dragon Warrior to Tanner's grandmother, letting her go. 'Then I will have to *make* you tell me.'

'You'll be rotting in your grave before I tell you anything,' shouted Esme.

The Dragon Warrior gave a small nod, and the soldiers advanced. Tanner swung his sword, but the blow was parried by a spear and the blade thrown from his hand. A soldier gripped Tanner's throat and tripped him backwards. White light filled his eyes as his head slammed into the hard ground. He felt cold iron across his throat. A knife.

'You will tell us,' the Dragon Warrior said. 'Or it's the boy's blood we'll spill.'

'All right,' Esme said despairingly. 'Don't hurt him!'

Tanner twisted his neck and saw his grandmother wringing her hands.

'Well?' said the Dragon Warrior.

'Promise you won't harm my grandson.'

'You have my word,' the Dragon Warrior said. 'Give me the mask, and he will live.'

'Don't do it!' shouted Tanner.

His grandmother was pale, breathing heavily. 'It's under the floorboards,' she said. 'Behind the chest in the kitchen.'

The Dragon Warrior nodded to one of his men, who ran inside the cottage. Tanner heard him throwing the chest aside. Where was Firepos?

I need you now. He sent a message out to his Beast, closing his eyes in concentration.

I sweep down, hurling a fireball at Varlot's head. He lifts his armoured arm and the flames smash across it, making him roar. He stumbles backwards in pain. I pound him again, and the fireball breaks over his back, knocking him to his knees. I can hold him off for a time, but not for long.

Screams rise up from the square. The enemy are being held, but brave men and women are lying wounded or dead. The invaders are relentless in their ferocity. The owner rushes out from the bakery where Tanner works.

'Cowards!' he shouts at the soldiers. He grasps a long wooden pole ending in a metal shovel and thrusts it into the neck of an enemy soldier. The man collapses, clutching at his throat. But two soldiers leap on the baker, and he falls against a wall. They stab him, and he groans his last breath.

Pain shoots up my wing. I drop, almost hitting a

thatched roof, but pull clear, despite the agony. Another arrow thuds into my belly. I see a soldier with a longbow, aiming another arrow at me. He shoots.

I dip my wing and dodge the shaft. I am wounded, but not enough to stop me. Gathering a fireball, I fling it towards him. The thatch blazes and he falls through into the cottage below with a scream.

Tanner needs me! I feel it like the pain of the arrows, but deeper.

The soldier came running out of the house. In his hands, he held a piece of sackcloth.

'I've found it, General Gor!' he said. 'But...'

So that's his name, thought Tanner.

'Give it to me!' General Gor said. He snatched the object from his hand, and crouched down. He tipped out the contents onto the ground.

'What's this?' he bellowed.

'I tried to tell you, sir...'

Tanner managed to catch a glimpse of what had been in the sack. It was only a piece of the mask –

an eye socket, part of the upper brow with a twisted horn, and a loose piece of jowl. He remembered it well.

Gor thrust the fragment into Esme's face. 'Where is the rest of it?' he barked, spittle flying from his lips.

Esme paused, and her eyes met Tanner's. The look lasted only a heartbeat, but it spoke more than words. She shook her head. 'That's all I have.'

Gor turned and looked at Tanner with narrowed eyes. His lips curled into a thin smile.

'Then you are no more use to me,' he muttered. He swivelled round, driving his sword through Esme's midriff. The point, dripping gore, burst from her back. Grandmother Esme let out a choking cry and crumpled to the ground. Tanner writhed beneath the dagger-blade, tears misting his eyes, until he found his voice.

'No!' he cried, and the word turned into a howl of despair.

Gor turned to his men as he tugged his sword

free. 'The fun's over. We have what we need.'

A soldier swung his foot hard into Tanner's ribs. He grunted and rolled into a ball. With his face in the dirt, he watched the boots of the enemy soldiers march away.

Coughing and clutching his side, Tanner crawled across the ground. 'Grandmother?' he whimpered.

She was half-sitting against the steps, her lips pulled back in a grimace of pain and her hands trying to staunch the flow of blood from her stomach.

He pressed a fold of her shawl over the wound, but blood darkened it at once. He could feel her pulse pumping blood from her body. Tanner gently brushed the hair from his grandmother's eyes and supported her head with his arm.

'I'll bind your wound,' he said, trying to reassure her, trying not to let his own fear frighten her. 'You'll have to tell me the right herbs to use.'

'Too late for herbs, boy.' His grandmother's face twisted with pain. Blood pulsed faster from her wound, soaking the shawl. She held up one knotty hand to stroke Tanner's cheek. 'The messages I saw in the bones are clear to me now,' she went on, every word an effort. 'A creature of great evil is directing Gor. It wants the Mask of Death. It must not find it! Death and ruin will befall the land...' Blood stained her teeth, and coughing racked her body.

Overwhelmed with grief, Tanner could find no words to comfort her. All he could do was gaze helplessly as her face drained of colour, his hand clasping her fragile fingers.

He heard a rustle from behind some nearby bushes. *Has Firepos come?* he wondered. But there was no one there.

Esme gathered the last of her strength. 'You must fight.' Her voice was so weak that Tanner had to bend close to hear. 'Go to Colweir.'

'Colweir?' It was a town to the east. He knew nobody there.

She fumbled for Tanner's hand and gripped it with surprising strength. Her blood felt sticky against his fingers.

'Find...the Mapmaker,' she hissed.

Tanner felt as if his limbs were on fire, and darkness swirled over his eyes. It was as though the past was repeating itself: first his father, now his grandmother. Her grip loosened and her hand fell away from him. Her head was suddenly heavy in his hand.

Esme was dead.

Tanner mourns the passing of Esme

Chapter Five

A breeze blew across the front of the cottage, carrying distant shouts from the village. The sounds of battle faded and stopped. Their work done, the raiders had departed.

Wiping the tears from his eyes, Tanner lifted his grandmother's body – she was little more than skin and bones – and carried her indoors, carefully arranging her in front of the fire.

His grandmother's box of oracle bones was lying near the table. Tanner lashed a foot towards it, scattering the pieces of bone across the floor.

So much for reading the future!

Gathering himself, he fetched a blanket from his grandmother's bedroom and draped it over her body. He sank onto the floor beside her, reaching out for his grandmother's hand, holding it in his lap. The flesh was already cooling. Her fingernails were yellow and ragged from a lifetime's hard work.

For eight years she's been like a mother to me, and

this is how I repay her: by letting her die!

Through the haze of grief, he heard her last words again. *Go to Colweir. Find the Mapmaker.* But who *was* the Mapmaker? What did he have to do with the mask?

There was a screeching sound from outside, and a flurry of feathers. Firepos thrust open the door with her beak. Her gaze fell on Esme's body.

Rage flooded through Tanner again. He snatched up a copper pan and hurled it at Firepos. It ricocheted off the Beast's neck.

'Where were you when I needed you?' he yelled.

Firepos sank down onto her haunches, her shimmering gaze never leaving Tanner's face. He felt suddenly ashamed.

'I'm sorry,' he said. Firepos was holding one wing away from her body. Tanner saw the shaft of an arrow and leaking trails of blood across her feathers. She twisted her head, but couldn't reach it. Tanner's shame deepened. 'Here,' he said. 'Let me.'

Firepos laid down flat, extending her wing.

The vicious barb had burst right through. Tanner snapped off the arrowhead and tossed it away, then stroked Firepos's neck to calm her. Gripping the bloody end of the wood in one hand and steadying her wing with the other, he pulled firmly. Firepos shrieked as the shaft came loose. Flames spread over her wings, sealing the wound.

Tanner looked back at the house. He couldn't leave his grandmother's body in the front room.

He fetched a shovel from the outbuilding.

Tanner kissed Grandmother Esme's brow for the last time; he would never feel her embrace again. Passing a hand down her face, he closed her eyes. He took the piece of red linen she used to tie back her dreadlocks and wrapped it around his wrist. Then he drew the blanket shroud over her face.

'Farewell, Grandmother,' he muttered. 'Thank you for everything.'

After he had filled in her grave, he went back to the cottage. He didn't need much for his journey, but there were two items that would be useful – his father's possessions that Esme had kept. In her chest, he found the silver compass, polished to a shine. There was the Looking Crystal, too. It was an oblong of milky-white stone. When Tanner held it to his eye, the swirling white would disappear and he could see across huge distances clearly. As a child, Tanner had marvelled as he stared at distant mountains: the Looking Crystal made them look only a few paces away.

Firepos waited for him in front of the cottage. Tanner retrieved his sword, cleaned the blade and sheathed it in his scabbard. Its weight against his side made him feel stronger.

Tanner looked back to the cottage for the last time. Without his grandmother, it could never be home again. He trudged towards the village, wondering if he could do anything to help. Firepos took to the air, watching him from above.

A choking canopy of smoke hung over the village. The gates lay on the ground where the varkules had battered them from their hinges. Crumpled bodies lay still, their limbs tangled and torn. The shouting and screaming had died away; the only sounds now were the crackling of flames that leapt from every cottage, and the moans and sobs of the few survivors. Tanner fought down a sickness that made him dizzy.

He saw a man rushing from the well with a pail of water to treat the grievous wounds of a boy on the ground. It was Ben, his face sheeted with blood.

A woman, stomach smeared in gore, stared up at him from the ground with unseeing eyes. A few paces away, a child's body lay twisted in the dirt, golden curls matted with mud.

'Why has this happened?' a woman said, gazing at her dead child. She glanced up at Tanner. 'Tell me!' she insisted, anger flooding her cheeks. 'Why?'

Tanner shook his head. 'I don't know,' he mumbled, 'I don't know why.'

He turned on the spot, taking one last look at his shattered village. The fires were starting to burn out, leaving blackened shells where snug houses had stood such a short time before. Today's attack on the villagers was surely linked with the death of his father all those years ago. His grandmother had hidden a fragment of the mask that had brought these men here today. Why hadn't she destroyed it? Now, Esme was dead – and others, too. Tanner felt guilty to still be alive.

'Firepos,' he said, turning to his Beast. 'Take me away from here.'

My Chosen Rider does not know where to go. Grief has clouded his heart. He needs time. I take him to a place we both know well – a mountainside far from anywhere. The hours pass. Tanner grieves for his village and his last remaining relative: brave Esme, who protected him and taught him so much.

Tanner's pain hurts me. My feathers glow dimly, just enough to keep him warm as another night closes in.

We must leave at dawn. We must go to Colweir.

Gwen and Geffen are confronted by a Beast

Chapter Six

Tanner awoke early the next morning. Firepos was standing guard over him. He stood next to his Beast and gazed out over Avantia. In the west, a black smudge stained the horizon.

'They must be burning the bodies,' Tanner said quietly. Grief settled in his stomach like cold stone. 'We must honour Grandmother's last words.'

Tanner leapt onto Firepos's back. He felt relief at having a purpose which would distract him from the empty feeling of loss that gnawed at him. 'Up Firepos,' he cried. 'To Colweir!'

Wind whipped through Tanner's hair and clothes as Firepos hurtled through the sky. *Will the Mapmaker know I'm coming? What does he know about the mask?* Tanner wondered. And why did he have to find a Mapmaker, anyway? Esme had never mentioned this person before.

Colweir was two days' travel on foot, but soaring on Firepos would take much less time. He pressed himself into the sea of feathers, letting the Beast's warmth pass to him. Woods and fields sped beneath them in a blur. He hadn't flown this far east for many years.

Colweir was larger than Forton – a centre of trade for many of the western settlements. It lay on the banks of the Winding River, where boats could unload and pick up cargo. Tanner steered Firepos along the river's course, skimming low over the flashing water.

Tanner heard a distant booming, and as they rounded a curve in the river, he saw the sight he'd been dreading: Gor's army, threading its way along the riverbank. Tanner pulled his father's Looking Crystal out of its pouch and put it to his eye. The outriders seemed to leap towards him. Gor's forces were marching at double speed, their leader mounted once again on his Beast, now in the form of a black stallion. One of the varkule riders was pounding a drum to keep time. Tanner's blood ran cold.

Why are they heading for Colweir? he wondered with a growing sense of dread.

Tanner swept across the riverbank and followed the army slowly, watching them from behind a ridge of rock. Gor was definitely heading to Colweir. He remembered the rustle he'd heard from the bushes when Esme had whispered her last crucial words to him. He'd thought it was Firepos, but… One of Gor's soldiers must have been spying on them!

Of course! That was why Gor let him live: he suspected Esme had a secret, and that she would only give it up to someone she trusted. And only then when she was at death's door. *Did he kill my grandmother just to force her secrets from her?*

Tanner's grip tightened on Firepos's feathers. *I brought them here*, he realised. *They'll be after the Mapmaker too. Why did I delay in coming?* Tanner cursed himself. He'd already seen how desperately the general had wanted the other pieces of the Mask of Death. *If they've massacred one village, they'll surely do the same again.*

'We have to reach the town first,' he said to his Beast.

Firepos's wings beat faster, leaving the army behind. With the wind rushing past him, Tanner shielded his eyes to scout the land. Just ahead, between the fold of two hills, he spotted clusters of red tiled rooftops, veiled by smoke from their chimneys. Colweir. He shuddered to think of the people here meeting the same fate as those at Forton.

They crossed over lush, cultivated fields, full of toiling peasants. A man – Tanner guessed he must be the landowner – was directing them from his horse. They were in the path of Gor's army. Tanner pushed on Firepos's neck; a signal to go lower. As they swept over the peasants' heads, he called out. 'Back to the town! Run back to the town!'

The peasants stared up in astonishment. One or two dropped their tools; these people had never seen a Beast before. Some might have recognised them from stories and pictures – the Beasts of

Avantia were well known in legends. Tanner knew that few believed that these creatures really existed, and the occasional sightings that had occurred over the years were usually dismissed as fanciful tales, or the result of too much ale!

Tanner made another pass, waving at the peasants. 'Flee back to your town and close the gates. An army approaches!'

The man on horseback motioned to his workers to head to Colweir. They obeyed, glancing with frightened eyes at Firepos. Tanner suspected it was not his order but the sight of Firepos that made them run, but the effect was what he wanted. The horseman turned his mount towards the river and cantered off. Tanner turned Firepos round and swept over the peasants' heads. How long did he have before Gor reached Colweir?

They soared over the red rooftops, Firepos's shadow flickering below. Tanner spotted a man selling pies from a tray, children running along the street tossing a ball to each other, and a man perched on one of the nearest rooftops, mending the tiles. He looked up as Firepos skimmed past and nearly lost his balance.

Tanner urged Firepos into a steep bank. *Take us down,* he signalled to her.

The Beast dipped her wings and glided downwards towards an open cobbled square beside the river, which ran past the edge of the town. A wide wooden bridge spanned the water – Tanner knew that Gor would lead his attack over this bridge.

Market stalls were set up in the square. On the far bank stood a watermill, its large waterwheel churning up the rapid current. Beside it, a man was unloading sacks from a pack-mule.

The villagers in the market scattered out of the way and cried out as the magnificent Flame Bird descended into their midst, her talons scraping and sparking on the cobblestones. Tanner could only imagine what it must be like for these people to see her for the first time: her feathers rippling like molten gold, her hooked beak like polished amber.

'Do not be afraid!' he called. 'She won't harm you.'

The townsfolk who had not fled, cautiously peered out from behind their stalls. With tentative steps, they began to emerge, staring and muttering nervously to each other. A few of them inched closer. Firepos settled onto her haunches, trying to make herself look as non-threatening as possible.

A girl of sTanner's age, her hair so fair it was almost white, walked up to Firepos, her face lit up with curiosity.

'Gwen, no!' shouted a boy from where he cowered behind an overturned barrel. He was as fair as the girl and had an identical curl to his lip.

'I'll be fine, Geffen,' the girl replied.

They must be twins, Tanner thought.

Gwen stretched out her hand to stroke the Flame Bird's gleaming feathers. Tanner wasn't sure whether he would have been so brave. The girl smiled up at him. 'She's beautiful.'

Firepos gave her a friendly nudge with her beak.

Taking courage from Gwen's example, the villagers formed a circle around Tanner and Firepos. They kept a safe distance, but were obviously fascinated by the Beast and her strange rider. Relieved that the villagers had accepted them, Tanner scrambled upright onto Firepos's back. He cupped his hands round his mouth and shouted, 'You must leave Colweir! An army approaches. They destroyed my village and killed everyone.'

The townspeople looked at each other, then back up at Tanner, but none of them made a move.

'What are you talking about?' a plump stallholder scoffed. 'What tall tale is this?'

Tanner's eyes flickered west. How close was Gor? He remembered the horror of Forton – he did not need to imagine the terror these people would feel when the varkules ran into the square, tearing at everyone with their dagger-like teeth. *It must not happen here as well!*

'You're trying to scare us out of our town.' A tall man pushed his way to the front and gave Tanner a hostile glare. 'Then you can take what you want.'

'No! Just listen to me...' Tanner began to protest.

An older woman in a white apron stepped out from behind a baker's stall to address the crowd. 'What are you waiting for, you cowards? Run this boy and his unnatural creature out of our town!'

A chorus of agreement followed her words.

'Get out now!' someone yelled.

'You don't understand,' shouted Tanner. 'If you don't do something...' He was drowned out by angry shouts. The crowd began to advance. Firepos stood up and unfurled her wings.

The sound of a galloping horse thundering over the bridge caused a few villagers to turn. Tanner saw that it was the horseman from the field. His face was grim as he pulled his horse to a halt in front of the crowd. 'Gather your weapons,' he shouted. 'An army is on its way.'

A war horn sounds nearby. I hear trampling footsteps, and turn to see soldiers rounding a corner of the road on the other side of the bridge. Their leather armour shines dully. Their spear tips glint silver. Their faces are unreadable behind their helmets. The varkules lope on ahead, drooling with thirst for blood. Behind their ranks, taller than them all, is Gor. He sits astride Varlot, who lurks inside the form of a horse.

I let out a screech of warning.

The attack on Colweir begins

Chapter Seven

Cries of terror rose from the townsfolk as they pointed at the advancing forces amassed on the other side of the bridge. The enemy were chanting a war cry: 'Death has come, death has come...'

The crowd surged around Firepos, clamouring for the safety of their homes. The fair-haired twins were swallowed in a sea of panic.

I'm too late, Tanner thought with horror. *This is all my fault.*

As he watched the enemy approach the bridge, a sudden thought came to him. There *was* something he could do! Tanner scanned the riverbank and saw only the one wooden bridge. Even if he couldn't stop Gor, he could slow him down and give the townspeople a fighting chance.

'Up, Firepos!' he cried.

The Flame Bird crouched, then leapt into the air. She knew what he was planning and wheeled towards the river. The first of the varkules loped onto the bridge, followed by a company of spearmen.

'Burn the bridge!' Tanner shouted.

The townspeople gasped as the glow of a fireball flickered into life beneath Firepos. Tanner felt its heat and heard it crackle. On the other side of the river, Gor's stallion reared, its eyes rolling back in its head. Captains in the army barked orders and the men raised their shields to protect themselves from Firepos's missile.

We're not coming for you, thought Tanner grimly. *Not yet.*

With a shrill cry, Firepos launched her fireball. Tanner watched as it arced towards the ground, trailing a blazing stream of fire behind it. The land was suddenly bathed in a wash of orange. Everyone – Gor, his soldiers and the townspeople – stared in horrified amazement. With an ear-splitting crack, it collided with the centre of the bridge. Wooden planks shattered and were sent spinning through the air. The bridge, varkules and soldiers were engulfed in flames.

Those who were not incinerated threw themselves, screaming, into the water. But that didn't save them; the fireball was so intense it heated up the water, boiling them alive.

When the smoke and steam cleared, Tanner saw the bridge was in ruins, with the remains of Gor's army still on the other side of the river from Colweir.

In the town square, the crowd cheered.

But Tanner knew this was only the beginning. Gor had another weapon.

Varlot, still in horse form, trotted to the front of the army, in full view of the villagers in the square. He snorted louder than any normal horse could.

The crowd's cheers died in their throats – they could tell this was no ordinary animal. They watched, fresh fear growing within them, as the horse's rear hooves doubled, then tripled in size, hardening to bronze blades, and its bristling coat darkened.

Tanner didn't wait to see the rest. He had to

marshal the defences before it was too late. He steered Firepos back to the market square, landing her on a flat roof above the crowd who were backing away from the river's edge.

'Gather your weapons!' he yelled. 'Line up in the middle of the square.'

But few were listening to him. The sight of Varlot struck terror in their hearts. Cries of panic rose and the crowd surged towards the houses, away from Gor's terrible Beast. 'Flee! Save yourselves!' screamed a woman, her child clinging to her.

Among the seething mass, Tanner saw the twins again. They were being pushed down a street off the square, but every so often the girl would turn and look towards him. The square emptied. Tanner watched them and shook his head. He turned to face the river.

'It seems we are on our own, Firepos,' he said, fingering the red linen around his wrist. 'If we can hold the enemy off for long enough, we might give the villagers enough time to escape into the fields.'

Firepos turned her head towards Tanner and nodded, cawing softly.

A noise alerted Tanner. He looked round in surprise, then smiled at what he saw. From the alleys and streets leading onto the square came the people of Colweir, men and women. Some hefted axes, some buckled on sword belts, others had armed themselves with pitchforks and scythes. In the windows and on the rooftops appeared archers and crossbowmen.

The defenders formed up in ranks behind a man with a serrated sword resting on his shoulder. He nodded at Tanner.

They are up for the test, thought Tanner, *but there are too few to hold off Gor's army.*

A roar sounded from across the water. Tanner saw that Varlot's transformation was complete. The Dark Beast pounded the ground with his hooves and his head turned from side to side. His armoured chest heaved. The bronze, sharp as knives, glistened in the light. The enemy soldiers were wading into the water, testing its depth.

Gor shouted something to Varlot that Tanner couldn't hear. The Beast stamped along the bank towards the watermill. He lifted his muscular arms and punched a hole through the roof, tearing out several wooden beams as if they were twigs. He carried them towards the river. Tanner understood at once: *He's making another bridge!*

Varlot laid the timbers down over the water, reaching from one side to the other. It would only allow single file passage, but it was enough. The soldiers were already edging along it towards Colweir.

'Up, Firepos!' Tanner said. He squeezed Firepos's flanks. She knew what he was asking of her. Jumping from her perch, she swooped at the advancing soldiers.

Varlot was standing in the river by the mill, water swirling around his hips. He gripped two of the water buckets in his clawed hands and tore them from their mountings. He thrashed his way towards the makeshift bridge, throwing up huge waves, then stopped, watching Firepos intently. The soldiers on the bridge steadied themselves and continued their perilous task of reaching the other bank.

'Attack!' yelled Tanner.

Firepos screeched as she dived at the soldiers on the bridge. They lifted their shields as flames flickered on the Beast's wingtips. Varlot howled, submerging both buckets under the water. With a grunt of effort, he hurled the water at the Flame Bird. Firepos tried to jerk aside but she wasn't quick enough. Water cascaded over her feathers, soaking them and dousing her flames.

'Cross the river!' bellowed the Dragon Warrior. 'Quickly, you dogs!'

Tanner spluttered as Firepos twisted away, gathering herself for another pass. He could see the glow of a smaller fireball reflecting off her beak.

But it was too late. Already soldiers were piling into the square and forming up into tightly packed ranks. Captains bellowed orders. Shields locked together and weapons were lowered, creating an armoured wall, bristling with spears. Eyes glimmered behind helmets. They waited as their ranks swelled further.

'Advance. Half-pace. Decimate them!' Gor bawled as he stepped off the bridge, followed by more of his men. Iron-shod boots echoed in perfect time on the cobbled stones. Armour clanked. 'Death has come, death has come...' they chanted.

'Loose!' the villager with the serrated sword shouted.

Arrows and crossbow bolts whickered out and clattered against the armoured mass. It kept Gor's men behind their shields, but they were advancing relentlessly, a pace at a time, and no hit was scored.

Firepos dodged a sluice of water thrown up by Varlot and released her fireball at the soldiers. It bounced off the ground and rolled through the middle of the advancing soldiers, scattering several and leaving a trail of fire across the ground.

"Hold steady!" shouted Gor. "It's me you should fear, not that Beast!"

"Death has come, death has come..." The soldiers continued their advance.

Tanner abandoned the attack on the bridge, and flew Firepos back over the soldiers and varkules heading for the villager's wavering line. General Gor's troops were closing the gap and spreading out, ready to outflank them, cutting off their escape routes.

Firepos streaked into the square, landing with a screech between the soldiers and the defenders. Tanner leapt off her back, drawing his sword – if this was where he made his final stand, so be it. He glanced over his shoulder at the defenders. They exchanged nods, as if to say, *We're with you.* Tanner faced Gor's advancing soldiers. *Time to fight,* he thought determinedly.

The people of Colweir defend their home

Chapter Eight

Time seemed to slow down. Tanner stared at the advancing soldiers. He saw an arrow pass through a soldier's visor. Blood spurted and the man dropped limply to the ground. The soldiers didn't even pause as their boots tramped over the corpse.

He saw the varkules loping at the edges of the advancing mass, spines bristling, teeth dripping with foul-smelling drool.

Fear gripped his heart and his sword was slippery in his grasp. Firepos took to the skies. Her departure made Tanner feel alone and exposed. Sweat dripped into his eyes. He wiped it off with the red linen around his wrist.

Gor's men were only ten paces away. Tanner knew that if they charged at once they would be defeated. Varlot emerged from the river, dripping wet. He seemed to be shrinking, and his hardened armour softened once more to fur. His arms were drawn back towards his body, then he fell forward onto the ground with a thump, a horse once again.

Why is he changing back? Tanner wondered, but he didn't have time to dwell on it.

'Ready?' he called over his shoulder. He heard grunts of encouragement and voices calling out their support. He tightened his grip on his sword hilt and brought the blade level with his face, aiming it at the line of infantry.

Tanner's voice rang out: 'Charge!' He broke into a run and heard the other men shouting behind him. Some pulled level, their cheeks red and eyes bright.

Gor's men ran to meet them, light flashing on their levelled spears. Metal clashed as the people of Colweir threw themselves against the invaders. Death-cries echoed across the square as many were skewered on the spears.

Tanner dodged between two shafts, driving his sword against the leather armour of a soldier, but his blade slipped against the polished hide. With a cry, he staggered to one side. The soldier dropped his spear and drew his sword, bringing it round in a wide arc, sending Tanner leaping out of the way, missing by no more than a finger's breadth. A second later and Tanner's innards would have been slithering around his feet.

Glancing up at the soldier, Tanner barrelled forwards, holding the blade out before him. It slid down the other man's weapon until the hilts jammed together. The soldier grinned behind his visor and twisted his sword, throwing Tanner to the ground. Tanner rolled onto his back, held his sword out in front of him and swept his feet into the man's legs, making him stumble and pierce himself on his sword. He slid down the blade, blood pouring from his gurgling mouth, eyes wide with shock.

Tanner struggled out from under him and pulled his sword free. He gazed down at the dead man, watching his life ebb away. *Another life I have taken*, he thought. *But I have no choice.*

A blow from behind knocked Tanner onto his back. Instinct made him roll aside as a blade descended. It pierced into the ground where Tanner's head had been an instant before. As his attacker tried to free his weapon, Tanner jumped up and sliced clean through his arm with his sword. The man fell screaming, clutching at his bloody stump.

A huge soldier with a double-handed sword descended on Tanner. His armour was streaked with blood, and he was laughing maniacally, battle-lust burning in his eyes. He swung his sword with brute strength at chest level. Tanner managed to step back, out of its path, but nearly lost his balance.

The soldier swung again. Tanner deflected the blade with his own, throwing off sparks, but the force jolted his arm. Another swing came, this time at his head. Tanner tried to lift his sword to parry the blow but he knew he would be too late...

A shadow passed overhead. Huge claws clenched over the soldier's head and he was lifted off the ground, muffled screams coming out of his helmet. Firepos hurled the thrashing soldier at a varkule. Startled, the beast turned on the broken soldier and tore him in half with his claws.

'Fall back! Fall back!' shouted the villager with the serrated sword, now slick with gore. His command was cut short as a crossbow bolt thudded into his chest, throwing him back against a market stall.

Tanner looked about. The defenders' line was broken. Gor's men filled the square, surrounding the last pockets of fighters. Bodies lay strewn and torn on the ground.

Firepos screeched from above and Tanner saw a fireball career into the enemy, burning a group of spearmen, and sending others scattering away from the flames. But still the forces closed, sensing victory. He found himself at the edge of a small band of defenders, all battered and bloodied. A contingent of spearmen surrounded them, weapons levelled.

It was almost over. He had failed.

'Cease!' bellowed Gor.

The fighting petered out. Tanner saw Gor trot forwards on his stallion.

Firepos hovered overhead, a fireball spinning in her talons.

'Call off the phoenix,' said Gor. 'Or everyone dies, and this whole town will burn.'

Tanner didn't have a choice. He raised his fist. 'Firepos, no!'

The fireball disappeared as the Beast tipped her wings and flew back to land on top of a storage barn behind the small group of defenders. She sent out a call across the square, ruffling her feathers.

Silence fell.

The enemy soldiers parted as Gor approached.

'Thank you for bringing us here, boy,' he said to Tanner, loud enough for everyone to hear. Tanner burned with desire to charge at the man who had killed his grandmother. But he knew the soldiers would cut him down before he made it halfway.

'You spied on me,' he shouted. 'After you killed an innocent old woman in cold blood.'

General Gor laughed. 'Innocence means nothing in this war.'

A young defender with dark hair, bleeding from a scalp wound stepped forward. 'We're not at war!'

he shouted. 'We don't even know who you are.'

Gor dismounted from his stallion, his armour clanking. From a bag strapped to the saddle, he took out Esme's fragment of the mask and held it aloft. Tanner felt as though some ancient evil was watching him through the empty eye socket.

'Until I have all the pieces of the Mask of Death, Avantia will suffer!' shouted Gor. 'I will not rest until my search is complete.'

'They don't have what you're looking for,' Tanner said.

'Oh, yes they do.' General Gor pulled off his dragon-snouted helmet. 'Bring me the Mapmaker!'

A chill spread over Tanner. So Gor had even overheard that part of his grandmother's final words. The dark-haired defender looked back at his comrades. 'What shall I do?'

A few shrugged, some nodded.

'Don't tell him!' someone said.

'Why should we tell you, you murderer?' the

dark-haired defender shouted at Gor.

'Ask yourself this question,' said the general, smiling and revealing a glint of teeth. 'Do I give up the Mapmaker, or do I condemn everyone I know and care about to death?'

'Don't listen to him,' Tanner cried. 'He'll kill you anyway!'

The dark-haired defender looked at his feet. Then his jaw stiffened. 'Very well. I'll lead you there.'

'Traitor,' a woman in the crowd yelled. 'You don't know what—'

A bolt thudded into her chest, cutting off her words. Tanner saw one of the varkule riders with his crossbow levelled. The villager fell to her knees, choking for breath. The varkule's rider clicked his tongue and the varkule leapt forward, its teeth slashing like blades. It batted the woman's body over and lunged at her throat. Blood spurted.

'Good work,' said General Gor. 'Call him off.' The soldier clicked his tongue again and reluctantly the varkule backed away, a ribbon of flesh caught in his teeth. 'Now, would anyone else like to object?'

People shook their heads; no one spoke.

The general's eyes fell on Tanner. 'You've outlived your usefulness.' He turned to a crossbowman. 'Kill him.'

A varkule outrider

Chapter Nine

Tanner didn't hesitate. He put two fingers in his mouth and whistled. Firepos swooped down towards him. As the soldier levelled his crossbow, Tanner jumped up and grabbed Firepos's claw. He was heaved into the air and the bolt thudded into a cart behind where he'd been standing.

'Idiot! You missed,' General Gor shouted.

Tanner let Firepos carry him a hundred paces, until they could no longer see the square, then let go and landed on the roof of a building, clutching at the thatch.

'I need to find the Mapmaker before Gor does,' he said to Firepos. 'Stay out of sight until I call you.'

The Beast spread her golden wings and took to the air.

Tanner lowered himself from the roof and dropped into the narrow alley. It was empty, and the houses on either side were quiet, although he suspected many were a refuge for the terrified Colweirians;

they had to be hiding somewhere.

He knocked at the first door he came across. He heard someone moving behind it.

'I'm not the enemy,' Tanner hissed through the crack. 'Please, I need your help.'

The door was flung open and before Tanner could move, something cold pressed into his neck. He stared into the eyes of a young woman, who gripped a gardening fork with white-knuckled hands. He winced as sharp prongs dug into his skin.

'What do you want?' she whispered aggressively.

Tanner put his hands in the air.

'The brute who attacked your town wants someone called the Mapmaker,' he said. 'I need to find him first.'

'The Mapmaker's gone,' she said. 'He left long ago. His apprentice is still here, though.'

'Where can I find him?' asked Tanner.

The woman narrowed her eyes. 'Why should I tell you anything?'

'He's in terrible danger,' said Tanner. 'Trust me, if

these murderers wanted to find you, you'd want to be warned about it first.'

The woman lowered the fork. 'All right. You look honest enough. The Mapmaker lived on the other side of town,' she said. 'Follow this alley, take the third turning on the right. Keep going until you find the butcher's. It's next door. There's a sign.'

Nodding his thanks, Tanner sped off down the alley, sprinting across open roads, terrified that Gor's soldiers would spot him. Lungs burning and brow slick with sweat, he peeked around a corner and saw the butcher's a few buildings down.

Next door to the butchers was a building with a sign above it: *Mapmakers of Avantia.* Two of Gor's soldiers stood on either side of the entrance. Tanner saw the door hanging on its hinges.

I'm too late! Tanner thought.

The body of the dark-haired boy who had led them to the Mapmaker lay spread-eagled on the ground, blood oozing from his slashed throat. Tanner darted out from the alley as quickly as he could and hid in the butcher's doorway.

General Gor strode out from the Mapmakers. 'Excellent,' he said. 'We have what we need.'

Tanner peered out from his hiding place. Gor stood barely five steps away from him, tall and imposing. Squirming in his grasp was Geffen, the fair-haired boy from the market. In his other gauntlet he clutched a rolled up parchment. Tanner stared at it. *It's a map!*

'This map will show us where to find the other pieces of the mask,' Gor growled.

Tanner gripped his sword-hilt, his skin prickling. He couldn't let Gor get away with the map.

'Shall we kill the boy?' said one of the soldiers, drawing a dagger from his belt. Geffen whimpered.

Gor gripped Geffen's collar and lifted him off the ground, regarding him coldly. 'Not yet,' he said. 'The Mapmaker may have gone, but his apprentice here may be useful. Besides, he might provide the varkules with some sport later on.'

The boy's eyes widened in terror. Gor dropped him and looked around with distaste. 'Let us leave this rat-hole. The smell of peasant is making me feel sick.'

Tanner followed them back to the main square, keeping a safe distance, his mind whirling as he tried to decide what to do next. He could not attack, but he had to stop Gor from taking the map. The surviving defenders were still in their groups, surrounded by Gor's men.

'Take him!' shouted Gor, thrusting the boy roughly towards one of the varkule riders. The boy skidded to a halt in front of the drooling varkule, pale with terror. The creature pulled back its lips and growled hungrily. Its rider dismounted, seized the boy by the scruff of his collar and threw him over the saddle.

'He's just a boy!' The pale-haired girl called Gwen ran out from an alley, gripping a poker. A laughing soldier lowered his spear as the slender girl rushed towards him. She ducked beneath the tip and swung her poker into his knee. He fell down with a cry, clutching his leg.

She lunged at the rider who held her brother, but more soldiers grabbed her arms and forced the poker out of her hand. She writhed in their grasp, shouting, 'Geffen, no! Don't let them!'

The boy looked helplessly at her, fear etched into his features.

Gor addressed the crowd of terrified townsfolk. 'If any of you are foolish enough to come after us, know this: we will kill the boy.' A grin spread across his face. 'And I shall see to it that our best torturer makes it a very slow, very painful death.' He beckoned to his archers. 'Burn it down.' He gestured to the village. 'Smoke smells better than peasant.'

Just then, Tanner saw Gwen rake her nails at one of her captor's eyes. He fell back, clutching his face. For a moment, Gwen's arm was free, but Gor stepped forwards and lashed her against the cheek with the back of his hand. She sprawled onto the ground, crying out as her face scraped across the dirt.

Tanner knew he had to take advantage of the distraction. He edged further out, wondering if he could get to the varkule rider and free the boy.

Gor's archers wrapped rags around their arrows and then dipped them into little pouches of tar hanging from their waists. A soldier with a flaming torch ignited each arrowhead, then they put the flaming shafts to their bows.

'Please!' shouted a man in the crowd. 'You've done enough. Leave us in peace.'

'Loose!' Gor shouted.

The archers released their missiles. The flaming arrows arced into the air, trailing sparks and dense, oily smoke. They landed on the thatched roofs. Ravenous fire consumed the straw. An arrow thudded into a cart beside Tanner, and the straw inside went up in an instant. Across the town, he heard the crackle of dozens of fires starting. Tanner felt desperate. It was like Forton all over again.

'Form up and march out!' bellowed Gor, climbing into his stallion's saddle. The soldiers regrouped in companies, boots stamping and armour clinking.

Gwen rolled over, angry tears streaking down her cheeks. 'Cowards!' she cried, turning to face the petrified villagers. She looked dizzy from the blow as she scrambled to her feet. 'Why didn't you help him?'

As the soldiers marched out behind General Gor, the people of Colweir were emerging from their houses and rushing to the river with buckets and pans. Tanner could see smoke rising up over a wide swathe of the town.

Gwen stumbled and ran past Tanner towards the Mapmaker's. He caught her arm and she spun round. 'Let go of me!' she spat. 'Who are you?' She had a purple bruise forming on her temple and a scrape down her face.

'My name's Tanner,' he replied. 'These men attacked my village, too, just the other day. They killed my grandmother.'

'*You* led them here,' she said. '*You* let them take my brother.'

Firepos alighted beside Tanner, folding her wings with a hot rush of air. Her glassy eyes reflected the burning straw. Gwen took a small step away.

'We'll rescue him,' said Tanner. 'I promise.'

'Stay out of the way,' she said. 'I don't need your help.'

She struggled to wrench her arm from Tanner's grip. 'Let me go!' she cried, thumping his chest with her fist. Tanner released her, and watched as she ran up the street.

'You can't take on General Gor's army,' he shouted after her. 'Not on your own!'

'Who says I'm on my own?' she called back, before disappearing around a corner.

Firepos flattened her body to the ground and Tanner hoisted himself onto her back.

We have to save Geffen, he told his Beast. *It's the only way to might make amends for what I have caused here.*

Firepos took off with a mighty leap and a sweep of shimmering red-gold wings. Tanner felt the blasts of heat from the fires raging below. Discarded weapons, severed limbs and dead bodies littered the market square. The cobbled stones were streaked with blood – Colweir would never be the same again.

The rooftops of the town fell away beneath Tanner and his Beast. On the far side, a level plain of rich pastureland stretched until it reached a range of low, wooded hills. Gor's army was heading out across the plain, like a black snake wending its way to cause more destruction.

'Hurry, Firepos!' Tanner urged.

Air streamed through Firepos's feathers as the two of them surged forwards, sunlight tipping the Beast's wings with flame-red colour.

Suddenly, a shadow fell over Tanner and he felt a shudder. *Rain clouds?* Glancing up, he saw a flat belly and grey fur above his head, almost within touching distance.

'What's that?' He shrank back against Firepos's feathers.

The creature wheeled away then dipped down so it flew level with Firepos. Tanner stared in astonishment; the sight took his breath away.

The creature was a wolf as big as Firepos. His lean body was covered with shaggy grey fur and his sleek head thrust into the wind. He gazed keenly ahead with piercing eyes. Behind powerful shoulders grew leathery wings, beating the air with slow, languid strokes. Four crouched legs ending in paws with ragged black claws hung in the air beneath him.

And on his back, riding with confidence and grace, was Gwen.

The Beasts and their Riders soar through the sky

Chapter Ten

A ray of light pierces this darkest of days: we have found Gulkien and his Chosen Rider, Gwen, a girl of spirit. Gulkien and I soar higher. Our task will be easier, now that our number has doubled.

'That – that's a Beast!' Tanner stammered.

'Well spotted.' Gwen's eyes glimmered with amusement. 'I told you I wasn't alone.'

'It's your Beast? It chose you?'

'I'm riding him, aren't I?'

Flame Bird and wolf flew wing-tip to wing-tip, matching each stroke as if mirroring each other. For a moment, Tanner forgot about the pursuit and marvelled at Gwen's Beast.

'His name is Gulkien,' she said.

The huge creature dipped his head to Tanner. Tanner wasn't sure if he was friendly; his lips were drawn back in the beginnings of a snarl, showing the gleam of white fangs.

Gwen leant over to whisper in her Beast's ear. 'This is Tanner. He's a friend...' She shot a questioning glance at Tanner. 'I think.'

Too stunned to reply, Tanner just nodded.

'And I am Gwen,' she said.

Tanner swallowed. 'I know. Does this mean you trust me?' he said.

Firepos turned her amber beak towards Gulkien and called. The wolf howled back.

'If Gulkien trusts your Beast, that's good enough for now,' Gwen replied. Her long cloak fluttered in the cold wind swirling around them, and Tanner caught the flash of metal at her waist. Her belt was lined with a set of throwing axes. Holding on to her Beast with one hand, she dipped a hand into a secret pocket in the lining of her cloak and pulled out a slender rapier with a cross-guard shaped like a gaping wolf's jaw.

'Then you'll help me get your brother back?' said Tanner.

'No, *you* can help *me* get my brother back,' she said wryly.

Tanner smiled, then gazed down at Gor's army, far below. He put the Looking Crystal to his eye and swept it over the marching column. He paused when he saw the white shock of Geffen's hair. His hands were bound and he was being dragged behind a varkule, slipping and stumbling.

Tanner stole a glance at Gwen. Her blue eyes gazed down at the army, her mouth set in a determined line. What were the chances of finding another Chosen Rider? It seemed incredible that this girl had a Beast, too. His grandmother had told him to come here to find the Mapmaker, but was Gwen part of the plan as well? There was no way of knowing yet.

Tanner and Gwen soared high above Avantia, tracking the army that moved quickly and with purpose. Gor took the lead on his horse, followed by the spearmen, swordsmen and the crossbowmen. On either side, loping ahead, were the fearsome varkules. When the wind turned in their direction, he heard the monotonous trudge of the troop's footsteps, as steady as a funeral drum.

The sun sank behind the distant hills and a single star appeared above the horizon, where the dark shadow of a forest carpeted the landscape. Tanner was sure that in the gathering gloom none of the soldiers would be able to spot the two Beasts flying just above them.

'So, was the Mapmaker your father?' shouted Tanner over the wind.

Gwen shook her head. 'Jonas isn't our real father. Geffen and I were abandoned as babies. We were left in a hayloft. He found us one night when he was looking for somewhere to sleep. He fed us and kept us warm – he saved our lives. After that, we travelled with him as he mapped Avantia, crisscrossing the kingdom for years. He'd been training Geffen and I to follow in his footsteps. He disappeared years ago.

He left a note saying he'd done as much as he could for us. There's not a day I don't miss him, but he never could stay long in the same place.'

'Why did your parents leave you like that?' The question was out of Tanner's mouth before he could do anything to stop it. He'd lost both his parents at the hands of Derthsin, but he couldn't imagine how it would feel to be abandoned.

Gwen's face flushed and she turned away.

'I'm sorry,' Tanner said. He tried again. 'What's special about the map Gor stole?'

'Did you see it? What did it look like?' she asked.

'I only saw it rolled up, but it looked quite big. And it was yellow parchment with a wavy black border,' Tanner explained.

Gwen nodded sadly. 'I know the one.' She pointed to an outcrop of rocks high on a hillside. 'Let's set down over there. We'll be able to keep an eye on Gor.'

Firepos wheeled alongside Gulkien and together

they descended. Tanner saw Gulkien's four massive paws spread to cushion the impact of landing. He licked his long incisors and lay forward on his front legs to let Gwen dismount. Firepos folded her wings, and Tanner climbed off. Gulkien padded up to Tanner and sniffed him suspiciously. Tanner was startled but he held his ground; his head barely reached the wolf's shoulder.

Seemingly satisfied, Gulkien rejoined Gwen's side.

The four of them settled down behind the rocky outcrop, which sheltered them from the mountain winds. Glancing down the hill, Tanner spied Gor's army heading towards the forest.

Gwen spoke quietly. 'Judging by your description, the map General Gor stole is the only one covering all of Avantia. Jonas said it showed the way to a hidden power, even though it looks just like an ordinary map.'

'He never told you what he meant?'

Gwen shook her head, not meeting Tanner's eye.

'He said I'd know when it was time. That the answer was close to my heart.'

Tanner felt cold, even though the wind had dropped. Should he tell this girl about the mask and the hidden power of the scattered pieces? 'Have you heard of the Mask of Death?' he said eventually.

'Only from the stories Jonas told us when we were small,' said Gwen. 'They used to say it could control the Beasts of Avantia. But it was lost, wasn't it?'

Tanner nodded. 'Deliberately lost, I think. I mean it was hidden. We found it after my father fought... Derthsin.'

'Derthsin,' Gwen shuddered. 'You've seen him?'

Tanner nodded. 'Yes. He's a murdering warlord. He killed my father and took my mother. I never saw her again... I fear she's dead, too. Firepos killed Derthsin and my grandmother took the mask, split it into four pieces, and hid them. That's what she told me, anyway. Perhaps she had help from Jonas. She must have known him, or why would she ask me to seek him out? Now Gor is looking for the rest of it – he's already found one piece.'

'Does he want the mask for himself, do you think?' Gwen asked.

'I don't know.'

Gwen frowned. 'Why would they have gone to the trouble of scattering and hiding all the pieces of the mask and then make a map to show where they all are?'

'You knew Jonas,' Tanner said. 'Was he ever... clever with his maps?' Gwen smiled and cast her eyes down, so that Tanner couldn't see her face. 'Tell me,' he said.

She looked up. 'It's true that he wasn't an ordinary Mapmaker. Perhaps there's something special about the map he drew.'

'Like what?' Tanner asked.

Gwen shrugged. 'I don't know. We'll need to find out – if we get it back. And we have to, don't we? We've already seen what those men are capable of. We have to stop Gor spreading any more death and destruction.' She paced back to Gulkien. The mighty

Beast lowered himself again, his fur bristling.

Tanner watched her swing onto her Beast's back. *I'm not sure we can avoid death or destruction*, he thought. Tanner sensed that things were going to get worse before they got better. *But what choice do we have? We have to fight.*

He strode towards Firepos, his hand gripping the hilt of his sword.

Firepos and Gulkien swept down side by side, and landed in the thick grass of the meadow at the edge of the forest. The dense trees swallowed up the fading daylight, and Tanner could only see a few paces into the forest gloom. The track the soldiers had taken was clearly marked though – the ground scuffed with heavy footprints. Branches had been hacked down along the track, as if the soldiers had enjoyed destroying anything in their path.

'We'll have to leave the Beasts here,' said Tanner. Gulkien growled. 'We don't want them to get trapped under the trees.'

'All right,' said Gwen, 'but let's just scout out

General Gor's camp for now. I don't want to take any risks with my brother's life.' She pulled up her hood. Shadow fell over her face and only her mouth was visible.

Firepos ruffled her feathers and hissed softly. 'I know, Firepos,' Tanner said. 'I don't like leaving you behind. But we'll be careful.'

Taking cautious steps, they entered the forest. Night was falling. The air was cool and damp under the thick foliage. Each snapping twig and rustling leaf made the breath catch in Tanner's throat. His mind was filled with terrible images. What if Gor decided he'd had enough of Geffen and killed him?

Gwen froze and held up her hand. Tanner stopped dead. Ahead, he heard the sound of metal on metal. Gwen put a finger to her lips and beckoned him to follow. They edged closer to the sound. Soon he could make out hushed voices. Tanner's eyes strained to see between the trees. He spied an orange glow. Fire. He smelt smoke. That was good – it meant the breeze was blowing from the enemy camp, and the varkules wouldn't pick up their scent.

The trees thinned out as they approached a clearing. The moon had risen above the forest, giving Tanner a good view of the enemy camp. Tents were pitched beside a stream, and several fires crackled. Soldiers sat in groups, eating from bowls, and the smell of roasting meat drifted into Tanner's nostrils. He realised how hungry he was. One soldier was running the blade of his sword along a sharpening tool, another was placing a bandage on his comrade's arm. The varkules were lying on their stomachs, asleep after the day's long march.

There was no sign of Geffen.

General Gor strode into view, still clad in his black armour. Tucked under one arm was his dragon-helmet. He had broad, coarse features, with closely cropped red hair and a beard. Tanner shivered as he saw the malice in his deep-set eyes. Gor paused by a soldier who was sitting on a log, cleaning mud from his leather boots. He grasped a boot and turned it over, inspecting it carefully. The sound of angry words rose in the air and the general took a step back, then planted his foot firmly in the soldier's chest, kicking him off the log.

'Clean yourselves up, you dogs!' he shouted. 'We have a long march through the Broken Gorge tomorrow.'

He left the rest of the men grumbling and walked off. Tanner and Gwen followed the general, carefully navigating their way around the outside of the camp, darting from tree to tree. They reached a tent set aside from the others, with its own fire blazing outside. Gor was bending on one knee before the flames, his eyes closed. This was too good an opportunity to miss.

'Now's our chance,' whispered Tanner. Gwen nodded, her mouth set in a thin line. He drew his sword silently, and Gwen brushed her cloak away from her side, pulling an axe from her belt.

'Come, Master!' said Gor suddenly. Tanner peered around the tree again. Gor had raised one arm to the fire, and his fingers were splayed. Slowly, he drew them together in a fist. 'Arise, Lord of Avantia!'

The flames flickered and flared, stretching upwards into a column, swirling around like a tornado, changing colour from yellow to green. *Magic!* Tanner put out a hand to hold Gwen back and the two of them watched intently.

The fire died back, shrinking to an unearthly blue glow in the shape of...a man. Even from his hiding place Tanner saw a head with scorched hair and a face lined with vicious scars. The vision's skin was blistered and raw; there was something terrible about the image in the fire. Something familiar.

He swallowed a gasp. Even with the deeply etched scars and the features melted by fire, there could be no doubt. He'd seen this face before, as a child.

Derthsin. The man who killed my father.

General Gor summons Derthsin

Chapter Eleven

'Greetings, Master,' said General Gor.

'Have you retrieved the mask?' hissed Derthsin's image.

'I beg your forgiveness, Master, but I have not,' said Gor. 'Only a fragment of the mask was in Forton, where it was lost. It seems that the meddlesome old woman has hidden the other pieces, with help from a Colweirian Mapmaker.'

Gor glanced up into the vision's rage-contorted face. He hurriedly continued. 'But there is good news! We have retrieved a map telling us where the pieces are.' The general smiled nervously, rounding his shoulders as if he was trying to make himself smaller in front of his superior.

The blue image briefly flared brighter. Tanner closed his eyes against the glare. It *was* Derthsin, communicating with Gor through the fire. How had he survived being dropped into the volcano by Firepos, all those years ago?

'General Gor,' Derthsin hissed. 'Do you wish to earn my displeasure?'

Gor shook his head.

'Burn every village, kill every peasant. I care not what you do, just get me my mask!'

'I will,' said General Gor. Tanner could see he was trembling. 'I just need more time.'

'Very well,' said Derthsin. 'But if you fail, I will turn Varlot on you.'

So the Beast was under Derthsin's control!

'Yes, Master,' said Gor.

The image of the warlord shrank back into the embers with a hiss. Derthsin had gone; Gor's time with him was over. The general climbed stiffly to his feet and retreated to his tent, emerging a moment later with the rolled up map in one hand and the broken piece of mask in his other.

It was time. Tanner edged closer with Gwen at his side. They were only a few paces away when Tanner's foot came down on a dry stick. Gor's head snapped up. He stared through the trees into the darkness. He was looking straight at them — or was he?

Tanner didn't move a muscle. He didn't even breathe. Beside him, he sensed Gwen holding still. The general's eyes narrowed. After what seemed an eternity his body relaxed and he turned back to the map, unrolling it on the ground and peering at it. He gave a low curse, then bellowed towards the camp. 'Bring me the prisoner!'

Two soldiers appeared dragging a whimpering Geffen between the tents. His face was paler than ever. The soldiers threw him down at the general's feet. 'Leave us,' Gor ordered.

As the soldiers departed, the general leant down and seized Geffen by his hair. He yanked the boy viciously to his feet.

Beside Tanner, Gwen raised one of her throwing axes, but Tanner shook his head. They might learn something useful.

'It seems we have a problem,' said Gor.

'Wh— What?' asked Geffen.

'The map isn't telling me what I need to know.' Gor pushed him towards the unrolled parchment.

Geffen looked at the map and shrugged helplessly.

'You know as well as I do that the map has something to do with this,' he spat, holding up the mask fragment. 'And you're going to help me find the rest. What are the map's secrets?' Gor's face was contorted with fury, all his attention focussed on the boy.

Tanner turned to Gwen and mouthed, 'Ready?'

She nodded, her lips pressed together in a look of grim determination.

'I don't understand,' said Geffen, his voice breaking. 'Jonas never taught me how to read this map's secrets!'

Gor snorted, and threw the piece of mask at Gwen's brother. It bounced off his chest and landed on the ground.

'You will tell me,' said Gor, 'or you will—'

Tanner felt Gwen's arm swish past his ear, and

an axe spun through the air. Gor jerked back as it thudded into a tree a finger's breadth past his head. She rushed towards Gor, who quickly pulled Geffen towards him, and placed his dagger against the boy's neck.

'Stop!' Gwen pulled her rapier from her cloak's lining, and held the slender blade to Gor's throat.

'Gwen!' cried Geffen.

Tanner advanced on Gor, his sword levelled.

'Another step,' said the general, 'and I'll slice his throat like a pig.'

'If you kill him,' said Gwen, her blade steady as a rock, 'you die too.'

'Then it seems we have a dilemma,' sneered General Gor.

Tanner's eyes were drawn to the map. The piece of the mask lay beside it. If he could only snatch them up...

A crunch – the sound of wood splintering. The ground began to shake.

Tanner spun round, lifting his sword. Horror

swept through him.

At the edge of the clearing, Varlot stood with bronzed hooves planted wide, his massive chest rising and falling beneath his scaled armour. He reached out and gripped the branch of a nearby tree. With one massive tug, he tore the whole tree from the ground. Soil fell from the white roots and leaves swirled through the air. Varlot roared and hurled the tree straight at Tanner.

Brutal combat

Chapter Twelve

Tanner dived out of the way as the tree descended. Branches and twigs lashed his face. He leapt back to his feet just as Gwen lunged with her rapier, the thin blade hissing through the air. Varlot was too quick for her and leapt out of the way, his bronze hooves smashing into the ground as he fell back to earth. Gwen pulled an axe from her belt and sent it spinning at the Beast. It lodged in Varlot's armoured skin, making the Beast bellow with rage. Tanner hacked his sword at the Beast's side, but the blade bounced off with a metallic ring.

Varlot lashed out with a hoof, catching Tanner in the stomach, sending him stumbling through the burning logs of the fire. He landed face down in the dirt. Pain flared in his ribs, but he struggled up. Gor was dragging Geffen back to the camp. In his other hand was the mask and the map.

'Don't tell him how to use the map!' shouted Gwen.

Geffen called something in reply, but Tanner couldn't hear.

Varlot tore a branch from the tree and swung it at Gwen. She ducked beneath it and darted towards him, hacking at the Beast's legs with her rapier. The armoured hide was thinner there and the Beast staggered back, roaring, eyes swivelling wildly. Tanner ran to her side, swinging his sword.

'Run!' he shouted.

'I can't leave without Geffen!'

Varlot crashed into a tree, tearing its roots from the ground. He dropped the branch and swiped his arm, catching Gwen on the side of her head. She sprawled across the ground and stopped moving. Varlot raised a deadly hoof above her body.

'No!' Tanner shouted.

Just then, the canopy of leaves above them seemed to press down, and a dark shape fell through, splintering branches. Gulkien, wings folded, landed on Varlot's back and fastened his pointed fangs over the horse-Beast's shoulder. The

Beast's cry echoed through the forest.

Tanner sheathed his sword and scooped up Gwen. She was unconscious. He ran, not caring where he went, as long as it was away from the camp. He heard the howls and snarls of the battling Beasts, and Gor's voice shouting: 'Find them!'

Gwen stirred in his arms, rolling her head weakly. Tanner risked a look back and saw points of light in the darkness. Torches. Adrenalin drove his legs, his arms were starting to ache, and there was a pain in his left side. Had he broken a rib?

A light appeared ahead, through the leaves in the sky. It was brighter than any torch and seemed to hover.

Firepos!

She was trying to guide him out. Tanner stumbled between the trees, tripping over roots, watching the beacon above. The noise of his pursuers faded away. Finally, he burst through the trees and out onto a track. Firepos, her wings burning against the black sky, dropped down beside him.

Tanner laid Gwen carefully on the ground. She managed to pull herself upright, and looked around, dazed.

'Where's Gulkien?'

Tanner pointed back into the forest. 'He hasn't come out yet. He was fighting Gor's Beast.'

Gwen looked wretched. 'First my brother, now Gulkien.'

Tanner picked up the sounds of soldiers shouting to each other. One called out, 'This way!' They were getting closer.

Gwen stood up shakily. 'I'm going to find him.'

'You can't!' said Tanner. 'Gor will capture you, too.'

'But Geffen...' Her face was creased with despair.

'If Gor was going to kill him, he'd have done it by now,' said Tanner. 'Our best chance is to surprise them when they're out of the forest.'

Gwen stared into the trees, her eyes shining fiercely. A shadow moved. Tanner drew his sword.

'It's Gulkien!' said Gwen, as her Beast limped

towards them. His fangs were dripping with blood, and he seemed to be keeping the weight off one of his rear legs. His leathery wings were covered in lacerations. Gwen threw her arms around his shaggy neck and buried her face in his fur.

'It's time to go,' Tanner said, hardening his heart. They had to keep moving.

They climbed onto their Beasts and took off above the forest. Tanner saw the flare of torches fanning among the trees. He shuddered as he remembered Varlot hovering over his friend. If it hadn't been for Gulkien she'd be dead.

'General Gor said they'd be marching to the Broken Gorge,' he said. 'Maybe we can lay an ambush there, and rescue Geffen.'

'It's the only thing we can do. We'd better get some rest,' Gwen said. Her voice was thick with fatigue. 'The army isn't going anywhere until morning.'

She directed Gulkien in a long, shallow dive towards the silver ribbon of a river. Exhaustion crashed over Tanner in waves, and it was hard to keep a grip on Firepos's feathers. His head felt almost too heavy to hold up.

They landed beside the water in thick grass, and Tanner slid from his Beast's back. Gwen clambered off beside him, wrapping her cloak tightly around herself. Firepos nestled onto the ground and Tanner lay against her warm flank.

Gwen was tying a piece of cloth around Gulkien's bleeding leg. The wolf gave a low growl as she tightened it, but she soothed him by whispering into his ear. Tanner remembered her last shout to her brother as he was being dragged away.

'Do you think Geffen will tell Gor how to use the map?' he asked.

Gwen shook her head sadly. 'He doesn't know how,' she said. Tanner frowned. 'I only said that because if Gor knows the truth, Geffen's useless to him. Who knows what the general would do then?' Her face became troubled. 'I didn't tell you everything before.'

Tanner felt his mouth go dry. 'Go on.'

'Well, I do know how to read the map's secrets. Jonas told me never to tell anyone else. Not even my brother. But now...'

She was fingering a gold locket that hung around her neck. Tanner hadn't noticed it before. It looked old and worn. Gwen took it from around her neck and held it gently.

With a nail, she pressed the side of the locket, and the top sprung open. Tanner leant closer to look inside. He saw a folded square of grey silk.

Gwen pulled gently at one corner of the cloth, and unravelled it. The silk was so fine that Tanner could see his friend's face through it. It caught the moonlight like gossamer.

'What is it?' he gasped.

'It's the only way to read the map Gor stole,' said Gwen. As she held it up again, Tanner saw it was the same size as the map. He saw shadowy outlines woven into the silk. Impossible to make out now, but...

'If I lay this over the map,' Gwen continued, 'new

markings become visible'

'The locations of the pieces of the Mask of Death!' whispered Tanner. 'Esme and Jonas must have hidden the pieces and made a map only they could read, in case they needed to find them again.'

Gwen nodded, folded the gauze again and hid it inside her locket. She clicked it closed and put the chain back round her neck, tucking the locket away.

'We must get the map from Gor,' Tanner said. 'Only then can we get the other pieces of the mask before he does.' He rubbed his tired eyes. 'But now we really must rest.'

Tanner lay back against the Flame Bird's warm feathers. As he gave in to sleep, his mind wandered back to Forton, and his grandmother's body lying cold in the ground. Why had she not destroyed the mask?

And now Derthsin had returned to reclaim the mask! What terrible power he would have if he gained control over the Beasts of Avantia?

Before Tanner could think of an answer, his eyelids grew heavy...

My Chosen Rider falls into sleep; I will protect him as long as I have strength in my wings and fire in my belly. Gulkien watches by my side. Together we gaze at the endless stars.

The stench of evil drifts around me, coming from the forest below. Beyond that, I sense something else: the Mask of Death. It calls out to my Chosen Rider. It's a call that I hope he never hears. His fate is to retrieve the pieces of the mask. But beyond that? I dare not think.

How can it be true that Derthsin is alive? I remember plunging him into the volcano, and the feather tearing from my side. Did I let my Chosen Rider down, all those years ago?

I remember Derthsin's last words. He swore vengeance on the two of us...

Gor's army negotiates the Broken Gorge

Chapter Thirteen

When Tanner awoke, the sky was slate-grey and the sun had not yet risen over the horizon. He rubbed his eyes sleepily. Shreds of mist were drifting just above the treetops in the distance. Gwen was awake already, resting against Gulkien's thick fur. There were dark rings under her eyes.

'I hardly slept,' she said. 'I couldn't stop thinking about Geffen.'

'We'll get him back,' Tanner replied. 'I promise.'

He stood up, wincing. His side felt like it was on fire. He pulled up his tunic and saw a deep purple bruise on his ribs. Tanner pushed it lightly with his fingertips, but nothing seemed out of place.

'We'd better not get so close to Gor's Beast again,' said Gwen, eyeing the bruise sympathetically.

Gulkien rose behind Gwen, yawning to reveal sharp white teeth. Firepos blinked and spread her wings, flapping them to stretch her muscles.

Tanner's stomach rumbled. 'Come on,' he said.

'Let's get moving. The sooner we get to the Broken Gorge, the more chance we'll have to prepare.'

Gwen gripped Gulkien's fur and hoisted herself onto his back. Firepos flattened herself to the ground and Tanner climbed up. His Beast screeched and pushed off from the ground, opening her wings. She caught a rising current of warm air, and swept down from their vantage point.

Gulkien flapped alongside, and together they turned north towards the mountains, leaving the forest behind. Tanner expected to see a sprinkling of orange campfires through the trees, but there was nothing.

'Perhaps Gor's letting his army rest,' Tanner said.

Gwen snorted. 'I doubt it,' she said.

Tanner lifted the Looking Crystal to his eye and peered at the distant peaks. During winter they were blanketed in snow, but now only a few patches remained. Tanner had come this way before, during his training with Firepos. The Broken Gorge was composed of three ridges of rock reaching from the mountains' foothills to the plains below. Two rivers flowed down from a mountain lake at the top. The ridges between them were sharp and crumbling, due to the years of wind and rain. Walking up the gorge was the quickest way to reach the remote villages high in the mountains. The view from up there was legendary, stretching far over Avantia. *A good place to plan your army's next move*, thought Tanner. *Was that why Gor was leading his men here?*

Suddenly, Tanner saw something: a cloud of dust. He pressed Firepos's neck with his palm, and she responded by swooping low. Tanner saw what he feared. Gor's soldiers. They must have risen way before dawn. At the front of the column was General Gor, holding Geffen in front of him on the saddle. *Keeping his prisoner close*, Tanner thought. He rejoined Gulkien's side.

'We have to speed up!' he shouted across to Gwen. 'Gor's already on the march.'

Her eyes widened. 'Is Geffen with them?'

Tanner nodded. 'We need to take a detour if we're

going to get past them without being seen.'

First Firepos, then Gulkien, tipped their wings and glided towards the ground. Tanner felt himself shiver. Gor's army seemed invincible and tireless, like a machine for making war.

By the time the gorge was close enough to see without the Looking Crystal, the sun had risen and warmed Tanner's face. Only thin streams trickled over the rocks from the lake at the summit, like blue ribbons draped over the parched and dusty cliffs. Tanner pointed to where the waterfall cascaded through a narrow channel from the lake.

'Let's put down there!' he said.

Gwen steered Gulkien, and he followed. Together they alighted beside the water. There was hardly any breeze, and the surface of the lake was a perfect reflection of the blue sky. After they'd dismounted, the Beasts bent their heads to drink at the water's edge. Tanner's mouth was dry too, but there was something he needed to check first. He lifted the Looking Crystal to his eye and stared down the gorge. General Gor's troops had paused at the bottom. He handed the Crystal to Gwen.

'Something's making him hesitate,' she said.

'The gorge is dangerous,' said Tanner. 'The cliff sides are crumbling away. Perhaps they're worried about a landslide and will go another way.'

Gwen looked across at him. 'And if they do, how can we stop them?'

Tanner tried not to let his fear show in his face.

'There are only four of us!' added Gwen, kicking a loose stone which rattled down the slope. Tanner watched the clouds of dust settle.

'There might only be four of us,' he said. 'But there are a lot more loose rocks around here.' He gazed at the crumbling ridges and slopes strewn with boulders, and Gwen's eyes followed.

'Who needs swords and axes?' she said, grinning.

Below, Gor's soldiers were beginning to trudge up the gorge, with their leader riding the front.

Time to end this, thought Tanner.

Gulkien causes a landslide

Chapter Fourteen

'We create what they're dreading: a rock fall,' Tanner said.

'But what about Geffen?' asked Gwen. 'He might be killed.'

'We'll have to make sure that it only hits the soldiers at the back,' said Tanner. 'When the rest panic, we'll rescue your brother. We can sweep down with Firepos and she can grab him.'

Gwen nodded, her jaw set tight. 'I'll take Gulkien up to the sides of the ridge,' she said. Gulkien lowered himself and she scrambled up. 'We can prise some rocks loose. Good luck, Tanner. And if this doesn't work...'

Tanner patted the wolf's flank. 'It'll work.' He smiled thinly, hoping he was right.

Gulkien growled and bounded along the lakeshore, heaving his leathery wings. He took off, climbing over his mirror image in the water's surface. Tanner watched him loop back and along the other side of the ridge, out of sight. He heaved himself up among Firepos's warm feathers and positioned himself on the Flame Bird's back.

'This is it, Firepos,' he said. 'Another test for me to pass.'

Watching through the Looking Crystal, he saw that Gor's troops were making steady progress up the pass towards him. For a moment, Tanner's gaze rested on General Gor, his dragon-snout helmet obscuring his face. Geffen rocked limply before him in the saddle, his eyes closed.

He heard distant shouts echoing up the narrow valley. The image blurred as he jerked the Looking Crystal round. Some fifty paces behind Gor, a group of soldiers were pointing up the slope. Scanning the Looking Crystal up the gorge wall, he saw dust clouds billowing out – rocks and a huge boulder tumbled down the slopes. Tanner nearly let out a cheer as the rock fall engulfed the rearmost portions of the column, crushing dozens of soldiers.

At the top of the ridge stood Gulkien, his shoulder

braced against another rock. Gwen watched closely as the clouds of dust settled on the blood-streaked faces of the soldiers pulling themselves free of the boulders.

Gulkien heaved his weight against the second rock. Even from this distance, Tanner could see the muscles working beneath his thick fur. With a final effort, the rock tipped over the edge, plunging towards the panicking army. A heartbeat later, the soldiers' screams reached his ears. The men at the rear of the formation scattered: some threw themselves out of the way; others were hurled to the ground. The sudden rock fall had the desired effect: the rest of the soldiers stopped marching and scrambled back, gazing up at the mountain.

Tanner heard General Gor calling them into line, but another rock crashed down from the top of the ridge. Tanner saw Gulkien's leathery wings flapping as he tore at the crumbling lip with his claws. Gwen gripped his back.

As each landslide gathered pace, it loosened

more of the stones, sending smaller ones showering onto the exposed soldiers. Tanner put the Looking Crystal away and steadied his nerves.

'Ready, Firepos?' he called.

The loyal Beast spread her wings, and flames flickered across her feathers. She screeched and leapt from her perch.

I glide between the sides of the gorge towards the carnage below. Many are dead already, their weak human flesh no match for hurtling stone. Gulkien, my old friend, you have done well.

We head straight for the boy, who sits astride the stallion with the Dragon Warrior. They are facing back towards the panicked army, and cannot see me coming. I long to tear at Derthsin's servant with my beak and talons, but this is not the time.

We close, and I see the boy turn towards me. I am only a feather's length above the ground. His mouth opens in a gasp. I tilt my wings and lift my claws towards him. Don't be afraid, I am here for you.

*

General Gor suddenly twisted in the saddle. With one hand he shoved Geffen roughly from the stallion's back, and something silver flashed in the other. *A sword!*

Tanner tried to pull Firepos away, but the Flame Bird gave a cry of agony. As they climbed, Tanner looked back and saw bloodied feathers falling away from her belly. Gor leapt from the saddle, brandishing his sword. Beside him, the stallion began to change, rearing up on its hind legs.

Firepos juddered beneath Tanner. She was heading straight for the side of the gorge. He couldn't see how badly she was injured, but beads of blood continued to fall, splashing on the rocks. Her beak dipped weakly.

'Come on, Firepos!' shouted Tanner, tugging at her feathers, willing her to gain height.

The rock face loomed closer. Dread filled Tanner – if they hit the gorge, they would be killed. He pulled desperately at the Flame Bird's neck, and this time her head lifted a fraction. With a mighty flap of her wings, she gained a few feet and cleared the ridge wall. Tanner gave a whoop of delight.

'You did it!' he shouted.

Gulkien fell in beside them, gliding wing tip to wing tip with Firepos.

'We have to go back for Geffen!' Gwen called. 'Can Firepos make it?'

The Beast screeched defiantly and flapped harder, gaining height.

'I think that's your answer,' said Tanner. Flames burst from the Beast's belly and the drip of blood slowly ceased. She was healing herself.

They circled and broke over the ridge again. Tanner looked down into the valley. Varlot was standing with his hooves planted either side of the path. He looked bigger than ever, his face twisting to reveal huge yellow teeth, his bronze hooves stamping in the dirt. The scales of his armour glittered across his chest.

Gor marched with his sword drawn, pushing

Geffen ahead of him. The boy stumbled on the path. A ragged column of soldiers followed. Some were injured and were being carried by their comrades. Only one varkule rider remained, bringing up the rear. Each one of Varlot's massive steps reverberated in the gorge, shaking free loose rocks.

'We need to finish them off,' shouted Gwen. 'I'll keep Varlot busy.'

She urged her Beast down; Gulkien folded his wings and landed softly on the mountainside. In a blur of motion, he leapt down the incline, bounding from rock to rock, never missing a step. With his teeth bared, he charged at Gor's Beast. Gwen hunched over his neck, an axe ready in her hand. Gulkien leapt, eyes blazing as he slammed into Varlot's chest.

The Beasts crashed to the ground, cleaving a path through the soldiers. Gwen jumped out of the ferocious melee and circled, waiting for an opportunity to throw an axe at Varlot.

Gor's soldiers scattered in all directions as the Beasts rolled and thrashed in a blur of gnashing teeth and flailing claws. Gulkien sank his fangs into Varlot's neck, snarling and shaking his head to drive his teeth further in. Varlot staggered to his feet. He threw his head back and roared with a mixture of pain and fury. Rocks clattered down from above, hitting Gulkien on the back. With a yelp, he dropped to the ground.

With blinding speed, Varlot lashed out with a hoof, kicking Gulkien in the stomach and sending him hurtling into Gwen. She cried out, her face white with pain, but she quickly regained her feet and scrambled onto Gulkien's back.

'No one kicks my wolf!' she yelled in fury. With a fearsome war cry, she urged Gulkien back towards Varlot.

Tanner directed Firepos straight at Gor. He leant forward and shouted to Firepos: 'Get the boy. Nothing else matters!'

Keeping a firm grip on Firepos's feathers, Tanner swung his leg over her back and drew his sword. Firepos dipped low and Tanner slid off her back. In that weightless moment, as the ground rushed up to meet him, he saw Gor turn towards him and try to push Geffen out of the path of the oncoming Flame Bird. But he was too late. As Tanner hit the ground and rolled forwards, Firepos grabbed the screaming boy in his talons and soared away.

Tanner stood up, sword gripped in a guard position in front of him. His fear fell away as he watched Firepos disappear. His plan had worked!

'You've lost!' he said to Gor.

'Not while I have the mask fragment,' sneered Gor, touching the bag that hung at his hip. Tanner and Gor circled each other warily.

'You can't even read the map,' Tanner said. 'All this death,' – he pointed at the remnants of the army – 'is for nothing.'

Gor's eyes narrowed behind his helmet. 'I'm going to enjoy killing you even more than I did your grandmother,' he said. His sword arced, slicing the air faster than Tanner could see. Droplets of Firepos's blood flew from the blade.

Tanner struck back. He stepped nimbly forward, swinging his weapon in an overarm attack. But Gor was expecting it – he sidestepped and kicked the back of Tanner's knee. Tanner fell forward with a yell, twisting onto his back, just in time to see Gor stab his sword down at his face. Tanner brought his sword up to parry the blow, knocking it from his grasp. Gor's blade skittered along the ground, showering sparks. Grunting with annoyance, Gor stamped down on Tanner's sword-arm and drew a dagger, thrusting it at Tanner's throat. Tanner grabbed his wrist and slowed the dagger's descent. Gor pressed down. The deadly steel descended.

'My Lord Derthsin told me your father died like a coward,' hissed Gor, leaning over him.

Rage flooded through Tanner, lending him strength, but his arm was beginning to shake. His eyes were locked on the dagger. His sword was still lodged beneath Gor's boot, so he let go and scrabbled in the dirt by his side.

The cold blade touched his neck. Tanner closed his eyes.

His hand closed over a rock. He swung it with all his might into the side of Gor's helmet. There was a hollow thud and Gor collapsed. Tanner scrambled up. Gor was moving weakly on the ground, half-conscious. Tanner picked up his sword, raising it above the general's prone body. He stood with both hands gripping the hilt, the point aimed towards Gor's heart. *You deserve to die*, he thought grimly.

A howl sliced through the air and Tanner turned to see Gulkien collide into the cliff and land in a heap at the bottom. The wolf rolled over weakly, his fur matted with blood. Gwen ran to her Beast, shouting, 'No!'

Varlot staggered forwards. Blood poured from a wound in the side of his head. His body was covered in gouges. He stamped his hooves and bellowed, shaking the ground. Tanner lost his footing, and fell down beside Gor, his sword clattering to the ground.

'Kill him!' called the general, struggling to lever himself up on an elbow and pointing with a trembling hand at Tanner.

Varlot flexed his vice-like hands and strode towards him.

A time to rest

Chapter Fifteen

The fair-haired boy stands beside the waterfall and watches me, the orange glow from my fire flickering on his pale skin. His eyes are dark as coal. I cannot read them. At least he is safe. There is only one way I can save my Chosen Rider now. I let the fireball grow until it is heavy between my talons, then with all my strength I blast it against the crest of the waterfall. Splinters of rock fall away, and the path of the river widens, its current quickening. It is not enough. I shoot out more fire, and this time a slab of stone falls away. Water gushes over the lip like a flood. It smashes down the valley, scooping up shards of stones and carrying them down the channel. When it reaches the enemy, it will carry them away, too.

I turn and swoop down into the valley, with the water keeping pace below. Now it is a race between me and the flood. Which of us will reach my Rider first?

Tanner shuffled backwards as Varlot advanced, evil eyes glittering, his claws scything the air. General

Gor rolled onto all fours, shaking his head clear.

Varlot lifted a polished hoof above Tanner's head. He managed to roll aside as it smashed into the rocks beside him.

A distant screech filled his ears. To others it might have meant nothing, but Tanner knew every sound his Flame Bird made.

A warning!

Tanner looked up the gorge. A wall of foaming water cascaded down the slope, rocks and boulders carried before its unstoppable wake.

Varlot hesitated and turned his massive head. General Gor staggered to his feet. Firepos was flying faster than Tanner had ever seen her in front of the water, her feathers a shimmering red blur. She looked like a brush-stroke of fiery paint.

Gor tried to stumble away to one side, grasping the bag at his waist. Tanner took his chance and snatched it. Varlot roared and Gor lunged clumsily at Tanner. Then, Gor froze. Behind his mask, his eyes widened with terror as he spotted the wall of water as it hit him.

Tanner's mouth filled with grit and ice-cold water as he was knocked off his feet. His body rolled over and over. He couldn't breathe, his lungs were already burning as he clamped his mouth shut. Rocks collided with him on all sides. A sharp pain made his head explode and sent white stars shooting behind his eyelids. He tried to reach out to grasp hold of something, but his hands closed on nothing but water. *It's over*, he told himself. *I've failed*. All he could do was hold on to the bag he'd snatched from Gor, clutching it to his chest...

Long talons plunged into the water and encircled him. As the last of the air left his lungs, he was pulled free of the torrent. Before he fainted, he heard the cry of Firepos ringing in his ears.

'Tanner! Tanner! Are you all right?'

He opened his eyes. Gwen's anxious face was looking down at him. She pointed. 'Tanner, look!'

He sat up. From his view high up on the rock face

he saw water pour down the centre of the gorge. In the middle of the river, braced against its powerful current, was Varlot. Water crashed over his chest, he staggered backwards. His armoured hide was drenched and he was straining to keep his grip on a boulder at the side of the torrent, trying to heave himself free. Gor was nowhere to be seen.

Slowly, the Beast began to descend into the water.

'He's changing back!' gasped Gwen.

Varlot's head was growing smaller and his bronze hooves shrunk. Finally, with a noise between a roar and snort, the Beast was swept away. The stallion's hooves circled helplessly. Tanner stood up next to Gwen. His legs were trembling with cold. Firepos ruffled her feathers, heat pulsing off her. Gulkien growled as he folded his bony wings and licked his jaws. He was covered in grazes and cuts, but his eyes were bright with life.

Gor's army – the deadly force that had destroyed Forton and Colweir – had been defeated.

*

'And when she blasted the rock away with an enormous fireball,' said Geffen, 'well, I couldn't believe it. The river seemed to empty itself down the mountain. I've never seen so much water!'

Tanner listened to Geffen as they sat beside the campfire. His clothes had dried long ago, and they'd enjoyed a meal of roasted rabbit, caught by Firepos. The day's battles made every limb heavy. Firepos and Gulkien kept a sleepy watch at the mouth of the cave they'd found to rest in.

'I'm so glad you're safe,' said Gwen to her brother. '*And* now we have the map and the piece of the mask.' She brandished Gor's bag that Tanner had seized.

Tanner shuffled closer as Gwen unrolled the map on the floor of the cave.

Geffen's eyes were bright with astonishment as Gwen laid the silken gauze from her locket over the parchment. It shimmered in the fire-lit gloom of the cave and hidden features sprang to life on the map's surface. As Gwen shifted and settled the square of silk, Tanner could see pieces of the mask outlined on the map, the first beside a tiny drawing of his village.

Tanner glanced up at the others, smiling. His smile faded when he caught something in Geffen's face as he watched his sister.

Jealousy.

'The four pieces of the mask,' said Gwen.

'How long have you known about this?' Geffen asked, his voice thick. Gwen's face coloured.

'Jonas swore me to secrecy,' she whispered. Geffen nodded once, as though this confirmed something he'd always known. He sat back on his haunches.

'What does the mask do?' he asked.

'It gives ultimate power over the Beasts to whoever wears it,' whispered Gwen.

Geffen raised his eyebrows. 'Even those two?' He nodded towards Gulkien and Firepos.

'Yes,' Tanner told him. 'It's very powerful. If he controls the Beasts, he can take over the land and rule it himself. That's why we have to find the other pieces before Gor can give them to Derthsin.'

'We?' said Gwen.

Tanner was speechless for a moment. 'But I thought...'

Gwen smiled. 'Don't be silly. Of course we're with you. Aren't we, Geffen? After all, you helped us.' She put out a hand to her brother. 'You brought us back together.'

Geffen smiled uncertainly. The fragment of the mask lay between the twins – a grisly, ugly thing.

'Yes,' he said.

'Let's get some sleep,' said Tanner. 'Tomorrow we go further into the mountains. I'm going to keep watch with Firepos.'

'I'll be with Gulkien,' said Gwen. She drew her cloak and hood over her, and Tanner noticed her hand slip into the secret pocket to grip her rapier's hilt even in sleep.

Geffen settled down beside the fire, resting his head on his hands. 'I'll stay here.'

Tanner lay against Firepos's feathers, feeling the Beast's breathing lifting him slowly up and down. He gazed out over the kingdom. He turned to look into the far distance, where he imagined Forton must be. *Will I see my village again? Will I ever visit my grandmother's grave?*

In less than two days he'd lost everything he'd known.

'Well, almost everything,' he said under his breath. He still had Firepos; he owed his life to her. And he'd made two new friends to accompany him on his journey. *Will my journey bring me to Derthsin? It feels as though it is my fate to face him again. Are Gor and Varlot really dead? Derthsin cannot overwhelm my kingdom. I won't let him. I'll keep fighting for grandmother's sake. And for my mother and father.*

Tanner felt his eyes drift closed.

A noise made him jolt awake. He glanced back quickly, but it was only Geffen. He was lit up by the firelight, and was holding something in his hand, turning it over and over. The Mask of Death.

Images ran through Tanner's mind: his father smeared with blood; his mother, her mouth torn open in a scream; Esme standing in the doorway, an axe clutched in her frail hands; a girl with white-blonde hair, and her brother. And the vision of a familiar, cruel face that shone through flickering flames.

The night closed around him. *From the dark, a hero must rise.* Tanner curled up his body into a ball. The darkness was growing, and it filled him with dread.

Somehow, he had to find the strength to face it.

Epilogue

My Chosen Rider eventually falls asleep. He will need his rest, because his trials are only just beginning. Much has happened over the past few days, and he has suffered a great deal.

But we have found Gulkien, and his Chosen Rider, Gwen. That is a great comfort. If destiny is kind, we may also find Nera and Falkor. I hope to see my friends again. We will need their skills and strength in the trials that await. Until then, the four of us must fight on.

The battle for Avantia has only just begun…

Tanner's story continues in the Chronicles of Avantia book 2, *Chasing Evil.*

Tanner and Gwen must find the other hidden pieces of the Mask of Death before it falls into Derthsin's hands.

Will they find the next Chosen Rider and his Beast? And if they do, will he be a help or a hindrance?

And what deadly menace must they all face in the endless catacombs of the Hidden Mines?

Here is a preview of the next adventure in the Chronicles of Avantia...

Chapter One

Timbers creaked and crashed into the inferno, showering orange sparks. A fire in the building!

Tanner fell back, choking. How could he have let it happen?

The sound of laughter made him look up.

A shadow appeared in the midst of the fire. A dark shape moving. A survivor.

The figure stepped out of the flames. Black armour, cracked and smoking. The warrior wore a dark cloak and carried a sword dripping with blood. His face was pale, his brow heavy, and thin lips twisted into a sneer. One dark eye watched Tanner, the other was hidden behind a leathery piece of the Mask of Death.

Derthsin: the cruel warrior who had killed his father.

Tanner couldn't move as his enemy strode towards him. Every limb felt powerless.

Derthsin lifted the sword above his head, and the blade gleamed. 'The mask will be mine!' he bellowed.

Tanner knew he was going to die.
The sword swept downwards.

Tanner jolted awake. Stars were shining above him. Firepos stirred against his back, her warm feathers shimmering gold beneath the moon. She dipped her huge beak and rested her head against Tanner's shoulder. The forest below smelt like pine and wet dirt, and a moonlit mist hung in the air. In the trees, songbirds roosted. There was no wind to rustle the branches.

Derthsin wasn't here. It had been a bad dream, that was all.

The sweat cooled on Tanner's skin and he shivered. His Grandmother Esme used to say that dreams revealed deep and dark secrets. Esme was dead now, killed by Derthsin's general, Gor. Tanner had held her body in his arms as blood bubbled from her wounds and she'd told him with her last breath to find the Mapmaker, Jonas. Tanner hadn't found him – but he had found his apprentices, the twins, Gwen and Geffen.

Tanner thought back to his village of Forton, the destroyed home that he had left behind. *So much death, all in the name of Derthsin.* As a young boy, Tanner had watched Firepos plunge his father's killer – Derthsin – into the Stonewin volcano. But he had clung on to one of Firepos's feathers, tearing it from her, causing the Beast's blood to fall through the air around him.

Somehow, Derthin had come back to Avantia in fiery visions, instructing General Gor to commit terrible acts of violence in order to achieve one aim: to find the Mask of Death.

A few paces away from Tanner lay Gwen, with her head nestled in Gulkien's fur. The wolf's massive flanks rose and fell gently as the leathery skin of his wings lay folded against his body. Until two days ago, Tanner had believed he was the only Chosen Rider in Avantia, but now he had a friend with her own Beast. And what if there were more?

His grandmother had said that, when whole, the

Mask of Death had the power to control the Beasts of Avantia. Tanner swore to himself that this would never happen. They had already retrieved one piece of the mask, but they had paid dearly for it.

They also had the map that showed the location of the other pieces, scattered across Avantia. If they could find the rest of the mask, Derthsin would never have the power he lusted after.

But he has armies. And he has Varlot. Tanner would never forget his first sight of the evil Beast that spread chaos and destruction in Derthsin's name...

Tanner smelt a whiff of smoke and looked back into the cave. Gwen's brother, Geffen, lay beside the campfire under a blanket. The smoke thickened in low clouds and filled the air with the pungent smell of burning. Too much burning...

Tanner sprang up and ran into the cave. 'Geffen, get up!' he called. A glowing ember had fallen onto the blanket, which had caught fire.

But the boy didn't move.

'What is it?' asked Gwen sleepily.

Tanner flung Geffen's blanket aside, revealing nothing but a pile of firewood arranged in the rough shape of a body. Tanner spun round, his eyes scanning the cave floor. Where was the piece of the mask that had lain beside the fire? Geffen had been looking at it the night before, his eyes narrowed as he inspected the mask's thick, leathery skin, hewn from an ancient Beast's face.

'Geffen?' said Gwen. Now fully alert, she leapt to her feet, an axe in her hand. The braids in her white-blonde hair hung loosely.

'He's gone!' said Tanner, kicking the wood angrily across the cave. 'And he's taken the piece of the mask with him!'

Gwen rushed to the cave entrance, which overlooked the the trees beyond. 'Geffen! Geffen! Where are you? Come back!'

Gulkien bounded to her side. His lips curled back as he threw his head back and howled into the sky, his wings stretching wide. The wolf waited, his ears pricked. Nothing. He settled back down on his haunches and looked at Gwen, licking his lips. His eyes spoke his understanding. Gulkien realised that Geffen had betrayed them. How long would it take Gwen to accept the same?

'We have to find him!' said Gwen. 'He might be in danger.'

Tanner shook his head. 'Don't you see? He's abandoned us and stolen the piece of the mask.'

Gwen frowned at him. 'No,' she muttered. 'He wouldn't do that.'

'You must have seen how he was looking at the mask last night,' said Tanner. 'He waited until we were all asleep, then scurried off like a rat. The only question is why did he do it?'

'Why did you help rescue him?' she shot back. 'He's my brother – he wouldn't do this to me.' Gwen's face was pale and she looked out across the landscape, her eyes scouring the horizon.

She can't bear to look at me, Tanner thought. *But in her heart, she knows I'm right.* He opened his mouth to speak.

Gulkien growled at him, curling back his black lips to reveal fangs as long as Tanner's hand, warning him not to upset Gwen even more.

Tanner closed his mouth and looked out hopelessly over the forests and fields. Pink dawn was pushing back the black curtain of night, and pale clouds streaked the sky. Geffen could be anywhere.

'Well, whatever has happened,' said Tanner, 'we need to find him. And quickly.'

'Why?' Gwen spat. 'Because you're concerned for his welfare, or because you want your precious piece of mask back?'

'It's not *my* precious mask,' Tanner argued, 'I'm doing this to stop more death in Avantia. Or had you forgotten what happened in Colweir?'

Gwen shook her head in disgust. 'And aren't we all meant to be so very grateful to you.' She sheathed her axe, and went back into the cave. She snatched up Geffen's blanket, and held it under Gulkien's snout. 'You'll help me, won't you?' she said. The wolf sniffed, his pale eyes widening as he took in the scent. Gwen put a hand on the fur of his neck and he lowered himself so she could climb onto his back, nestling in his thick fur.

'You take to the air,' she said coldly to Tanner, still not looking at him. 'We'll find his trail on the ground.'

Tanner nodded, and hoisted himself into the space between Firepos's wings. The Flame Bird ruffled her tawny feathers. With a nudge from Tanner's feet, she spread her mighty wings and sprung from the ledge, falling for a heartbeat before climbing into the dawn sky on thrusting wings.

Gulkien, with the thin membranes of his wings pressed tight against his body, leapt into the scrub land, scattering loose rocks. With perfect balance, he half-slid, half-clambered down the steep slope, with Gwen clinging tightly to his fur. At the bottom, he paused at the tree-line, nose close to the ground. Taut muscles shifted along the wolf's back. His yellow eyes glittered like molten gold. He plunged into the trees with a spray of pine needles.

Tanner steered Firepos in pursuit, the wind buffeting him. The forest below was dark green and dense. They soared higher, cutting through strands of pure, wet cloud. Beyond the forest lay fields of yellowing wheat, criss-crossed with dirt roads and animal paths. Avantia glowed in the morning sunlight, grass rippling like waves. But nowhere was there a sign of Geffen.

Far below, Gulkien streaked across a forest clearing, leapt over a strewn boulders, then dashed into the trees again. Even if Tanner couldn't spot Geffen from up the air, the scent on the ground must have been strong.

Tanner's anger burned. *We've been through so much to find the mask. And now Gwen's brother has run off with the prize. Why?* He knew the power it could bestow in the wrong hands.

Beneath them, the trees ended. Gulkien paused, panting for breath. Tanner squinted into the sun. There was a shape moving in the distance — a figure running. Tanner felt in his tunic and pulled out his Looking Crystal. The oblong of opaque stone, inherited from his father, allowed him to see far into the distance. Lifting it to his eye, the swirling white faded away and a boy snapped into view. Geffen. Gwen's brother clutched the leathery fragment of Derthsin's mask in one hand. As Tanner watched, he disappeared over the crest of a hill.

Tanner swooped down, calling out to Gwen over the rush of wind: 'I see him! He's ahead. Follow me!'

Gwen pulled Gulkien's head around, and the Beast set off once more, racing with strides twenty paces long. They were approaching the low hill. Tanner urged Firepos and the Flame Bird beat her wings faster. He could sense the Beast's excitement. *We've almost got him!*

The Chronicles of Avantia
book 2

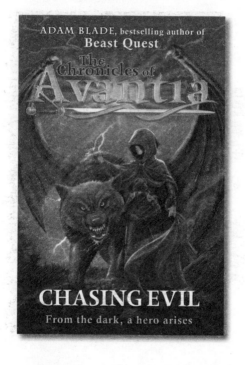

Chasing Evil
Out October 2010

The Chronicles of Avantia
book 3

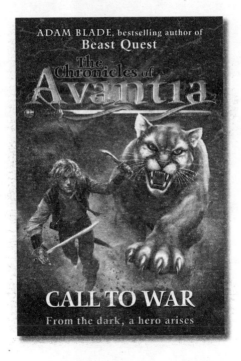

Call to War
Out February 2011

Other great books by
Adam Blade

The Lost World
Available September 2010!

Mortaxe the Skeleton Warrior
Available October 2010!

www.beastquest.co.uk